THE THEFT OF THE PURPLE PLUG

D0813211

By the same author:
Closing the Gap

The Theft
of the
Purple Plug

STEVE FLASHMAN

KINGSWAY PUBLICATIONS
EASTBOURNE

Copyright © Steve Flashman 1990

First published 1990

All rights reserved.
No part of this publication may be reproduced or
transmitted in any form or by any means, electronic
or mechanical, including photocopy, recording, or any
information storage and retrieval system, without
permission in writing from the publisher.

Front cover design by Vic Mitchell

British Library Cataloguing in Publication Data

Flashman, Steve
  The theft of the purple plug.
  I. Title
  823'.914 [J]

  ISBN 0–86065–795–7

Printed in Great Britain for
KINGSWAY PUBLICATIONS LTD
1 St Anne's Road, Eastbourne, E Sussex BN21 3UN by
Richard Clay Ltd, Bungay, Suffolk
Typeset by J&L Composition Ltd, Filey, North Yorkshire

Contents

1

The Jellybot's Tale

Every schoolboy knows that because of the way the earth spins on its axis, water in the northern hemisphere always disappears in a clockwise direction down the plughole. Tom was one such schoolboy, and so he was staggered when he saw that the water emptying from the bath was going in the opposite direction. What was causing this? Perhaps the earth had suddenly changed direction. Perhaps from now on *everything* would go in the opposite direction. We would have to change all the numbers on our clocks because the hands would be going round the wrong way. Everyone would be walking backwards, and cars would be going forwards in reverse gear. His imagination was running wild.

Mind you, there had been no unusual movement or earth-shattering sounds recently, so he was sure nothing had really changed. He put his red toothbrush back in its appointed place in the holder above the basin and watched the last drops of water find their way through the plughole in the bath. He was mesmerised by the strange patterns being created by the downward spiral of the water and felt as if he was being drawn in to its flow as it made its escape. Which, somehow, he was.

He had a sudden sensation of falling and turning. He remembered having a similar feeling while hanging upside-down, halfway through the loop on the big dipper at the local fair. Except he was sure he was turning rapidly in an anti-clockwise direction. And the familiar smell of the air freshener was replaced by the strange combination of seaweed and raspberry jelly smells.

There was a frightened yell and a scream of pain as he suddenly landed on a jelly-like substance. It definitely wasn't him making any sound. He had tried to shout for help on the way down, but no sound would come out of his mouth.

Tom slid gently backwards on his stomach until he came to rest in an upright position, as if he were sitting on a horse. But this was no horse. He grabbed hold of what looked like two rows of short black ropes to stop himself from falling any further, and he was suddenly yanked upwards at least one metre as two big eyes opened and a deep voice said curtly, 'Would you mind letting go of my eyelashes, young man?'

Tom sank back on to the creature's nose and stared wide-eyed and open-mouthed at the equally startled pair of eyes not more than an arm's length away.

'Who ... how ... wh-what are you?' stammered Tom.

'I,' said the creature proudly, 'am a Jellybot. You must be Tom! Pleased to meet you!'

'How did you know my name?' Tom gasped.

'Oh, I've been expecting you,' said the Jellybot. 'I'm so pleased you were able to drop in!' The Jellybot began to shake all over with laughter as he realised he'd just made a joke.

'I don't think it's very funny,' shouted Tom. 'Will you stop laughing. The vibration is shaking me off!'

It was difficult to tell from where Tom was sitting, but he guessed that the creature must be the size of a great whale — and it was probably of the same family of mammals judging by the smooth texture of its skin. The deep ruby red colour of its body helped explain its name and the sweet raspberry smell. Tom also detected other smells wafting through the air, the kind you would normally associate with a beach, and he heard the gentle, persistent crash of waves breaking on the shore.

'Where am I? What is this place?'

'I'll give you a full explanation soon,' said the Jellybot, 'but first . . .'

Before he could say another word, they were distracted by a loud commotion coming from the distance. Tom peered around him but could not see very far because of a yellowy mist that was hanging in the air. Out of the shadows, about twenty metres away, came three ugly creatures with hammer heads and tall muscular bodies. They had long hairy arms with smooth claw-like fingers, and their bulging eyes, which seemed to be stuck onto the sides of their heads, were wide with excitement. They were wearing big black boots, and their trousers were held up by rough looking braces. They appeared to be playing ball, but it quickly became obvious that they were throwing around a terrified little furry animal. With obvious glee, one of them started swinging the poor creature around by his golden fluffy tail.

'Put that Cosywag down at once!' roared the Jellybot angrily. 'You Clawhammers are all the same, always into mischief! When will you learn?'

The Clawhammers stopped in their tracks, and for one moment Tom thought they had seen him sitting on the nose of the Jellybot. But if they had they didn't show it. They dropped the poor Cosywag, who landed on his nose in a great lump of gooey mud. Then they turned and walked off again.

Tom had an irresistible urge to run over and pick up the Cosywag. Without a further thought, he swung his leg over the nose of the Jellybot, slid down to the sandy ground below and began running in the direction of the unfortunate creature.

'Wait!' shouted the Jellybot in dismay. 'I was just going to tell you about the minefield ...'

His words faded into silence.

Tom didn't realise it yet, but at any moment he could step on a spike which would set off an explosion of stones and grit deadly to any living creature. The Cosywag, gradually getting to his feet, looked up and blinked in horror through his big blue eyes at Tom's rapid approach. He watched helplessly as Tom's foot struck a cruel metal spike and his body came crashing to the ground. There was a deathly hush as they all waited for the explosion that would bring certain death.

But no explosion came. He had been lucky. He had landed *between* the spikes.

Tom lay still for at least a minute, knocked out by the impact of the fall. Although two other metal spikes protruding from the ground had pierced right through his striped shirt and another one through his grey school trousers, miraculously he was not too badly hurt. He felt a little dazed, but that was understandable in the circumstances. There was an unpleasant taste of sand and grit in his mouth.

'Don't move!' shouted the Jellybot, who was relieved that Tom hadn't been hurt. 'We'll get the Hummingbats to help you!'

The Jellybot began making a strange wailing sound, and within moments a humming noise filled the air. Tom couldn't see anything as he dared not move from his face-downwards position, but he felt the air disturbed by what he assumed was the rapid flapping of wings. The humming sound became deafening and Tom's hair began to blow about so violently that he thought it would be ripped out by its roots. He closed his eyes tightly as sand began to fly about in all directions. Then the belt on his trousers suddenly tightened as the Hummingbats attached a hook on the end of a long golden rope. Slowly and gently they lifted Tom from the ground, and with the incredible power of their tiny wings they carried him towards the Jellybot. Tom felt a little vulnerable swinging in mid-air, but it gave him his first opportunity to get a better view of things.

His attention was riveted by the sight of the Jellybot, now looking a much bigger creature than he had at first thought. His earlier impression of it being like a whale was only partly correct. It had a long smooth body similar to the largest mammal known to man, but it was much wider and dumpier in appearance, with a gigantic tail fin on one end. Tom was never very good at judging the size of things, but he reckoned the Jellybot must be at least twenty-five metres long, ten metres across at the widest point, and the height of a double-decker bus.

It had no visible means of propelling itself along on dry land, and Tom wondered how it got there in the first place. The Jellybot's face had a compelling attractiveness about it, and yet it expressed a hint of sadness. It reminded Tom of the face of a seal, although the nose was much bigger.

The Hummingbats lowered him gently to the ground, and Tom managed to get a quick look at them, too, as they sped away. They resembled the bats Tom had seen in pictures in nature books, with one big difference; their wings were transparent, and you could clearly see tiny muscular veins running through them and glowing fluorescent blue.

Tom began to feel very lonely and frightened. He wondered if his mum was worried about him, and if he would ever see his family again.

His mind was jolted back to the present by the affectionate squeaks of at least seventeen Cosywags who had followed their unfortunate friend from a distance to see what would become of him, and then carefully passed between the spikes of the minefield to join Tom and the Jellybot in the centre. Their golden coloured fur, big blue eyes and small round bodies made them look like fluffy toys that you might see in a shop window.

There was a pushing and shoving from the back, and through the crowd came Clarence, who was obviously one of their leaders.

'I want to thank you for showing how much you care,' he said, in a soft high voice. 'We Cosywags tend to be targets of fun for those louts the Clawhammers. Brutus is the worst. He leads everyone else on. We reckon he gets his orders from the wicked Megagrit!'

'Mega-who?' exclaimed Tom.

'Never mind about that now,' the Jellybot interrupted. 'We've got to get you cleaned up and prepared for the task in hand.'

'What task?' asked Tom, getting more and more puzzled.

'Questions, questions, questions!' said the Jellybot, who seemed to be trying to avoid the issue.

'Look, I refuse to do anything until I know what is going on!' insisted Tom in the firmest voice he could muster. The Cosywags glanced at one another and suddenly their big blue eyes looked tired and sad. They shuffled restlessly in the sand, huddling together in a mass of gold.

The story Tom was about to hear was going to set him on course for the most amazing and hazardous adventure of his life.

'We'll have to tell him sooner or later,' said Clarence to the Jellybot.

'Very well,' said the Jellybot, shifting his position slowly and deliberately to make himself a little more comfortable. It had been difficult for him since the waters of the Crystal Sea had subsided; his heavy body was not used to existing on dry land. He remembered with pride when he was the fastest creature in the water, and his agility was admired by all. Now his movements were restricted, and in any case he couldn't travel more than a few metres because of the minefield which had been sown all around him on the orders of Megagrit.

'Where shall I begin?' sighed the Jellybot.

'From the beginning,' said Tom.

The Jellybot started to tell his story. 'You have been brought here to play a special part in the greatest rescue operation our world has ever witnessed.' He paused for a moment to allow the magnitude of what he was saying to sink in.

'The inhabitants of this once beautiful land of Crystalan are slowly dying, because they have been denied access to the waters of the Crystal Sea which bring life and vitality. Many years ago in the distant past, the waters of the sea covered our land and brought life and laughter, joy and hope. Although everything had been provided to give a happy and fulfilled life, many of the inhabitants of Crystalan began to want more. They refused to admit that they needed the waters of the sea and they built huge dams to contain it, saying they would create a new life for themselves and drink the water when it suited them. Bigger and bigger dams were built, and the waters became more and more contained, until eventually much of the land became a desert and was taken over by the evil Megagrit and his Sandmen.'

The Jellybot paused for a moment and looked very thoughtful, as if he was choosing his words very carefully.

'That is why we are now facing the most serious threat ever to our existence.'

Everyone listened to the Jellybot with bated breath.

'You see, Megagrit managed to get possession of the Purple Plug which has ensured the existence of the Crystal Sea since time began. Although he cannot survive in water, he persuaded Brutus and some of the other Clawhammers to swim down to the basin of the sea and remove the Purple Plug. He told them it was the only way to gain true independence from the rule of the Rainchild.'

A wave of hisses and tut-tuts went through the listening audience.

'Although many of the Clawhammers died while trying to get the Plug, they finally succeeded a few days ago, and now the sea is slowly draining away. The inhabitants of Crystalan used to be highly skilled at moving around in the water, but tragically they have now grown used to the land. Many of our friends have drowned in their attempts to stop the water going for ever down the Black Hole.'

'I still don't understand what you want me for,' said Tom. 'I've got nothing to offer you. I'm nearly twelve years old, I've got a fifteen-year-old brother called John, a hamster called Hercules, and a fairly normal mum and dad. The only thing I'm good at is swimming.'

Tom's audience gave him a knowing look, but he failed to notice as he decided to tell them of his achievements.

'I've won certificates and I'm in the school swimming team and I came second in the hundred metres freestyle in our local water sports gala and ...' His words tailed off into silence as it finally dawned on him what they wanted him to do.

'You want me to teach you to swim!' he blurted out.

'Precisely!' exclaimed the Jellybot. 'Now the rescue begins!'

2

The Terror of the Black Hole

Tom sat down on a square rock and looked around him. He was a little bemused and bewildered at the sudden turn of events in his life. One moment he was innocently brushing his teeth, and the next he was in a strange world of Jellybots, Cosywags, Hummingbats and Clawhammers ... not to mention the evil Megagrit and his Sandmen! He loved adventure stories about the thrilling exploits of heroes saving unknown worlds, but now *he* was supposed to be the hero in a world of strange creatures he had never heard of before. It felt odd, to say the least.

The yellowy mist had cleared, revealing a strange confusion of sights. The cruel spikes of the minefield jutted out from the yellow sand, following a wide circular path around the Jellybot. Yet the beauty of the scene was breathtaking: a large natural bay, with impressive cliffs and a rugged coastline. The large beach sloped gently down to the sea, where sparkling waves left patches of silver foam in semicircular patterns. The air seemed fresh and clean, the sky was clear and blue, and the gentle warmth of the sun gave Tom a feeling of well-being.

He lay down on the soft warm sand next to the rock and closed his eyes.

Perhaps he would wake up in a moment and find that it was all a dream. There couldn't be any such thing as a Jellybot anyway! He had probably been thinking too much about his friend Sarah's birthday party. It was only a week ago and he could still see that jelly dessert. It was the most massive lump of wobbling matter he had ever seen! It had looked like a beached whale sitting precariously on the edge of the plate. He started dreaming about the fun he had had at the party, and a smile appeared on his face.

He awoke with a start to soft, high-pitched voices shrieking in his ears.

'Me first!'

'No, I want to go first!'

'It's not fair, you always get what you want!'

'Order! Order! I'll decide who goes first!'

Clarence the Cosywag was standing on Tom's chest getting everyone organised for the swimming lessons. The Cosywags were keen to get started. They were so obviously real that Tom knew he was wrong about this all being a dream.

'Come on, tell us what to do!' shouted the Cosywags in unison.

'First, we've got to find our way through the minefield and down to the water,' said Tom.

'No problem,' said Clarence. 'Follow me!'

Everyone got in line, and they were careful to follow in the footsteps of the leader. Tom was much taller than the Cosywags and his feet were bigger, too, so he had to be careful. He dared not step on another deadly spike — the next time he might not be so lucky.

He tagged on the end of the little procession and they made their way down to the shores of the Crystal Sea. The Jellybot could only look on from a distance; his body was so massive that he had lost all mobility. And in any case, he would never make it through the minefield.

Tom glanced back at the Jellybot. He really was rather like that raspberry jelly at Sarah's party. There was a squeal of pain as Tom stepped on the tail of the Cosywag in front of him.

'I'm sorry,' said Tom, 'I wasn't looking where I was going!'

'That was stupid!' said the Cosywag, ticking him off. 'You could get us all killed by your carelessness!'

Tom thought the rebuke was a bit uncalled for. After all, he never asked to be in this situation in the first place. But then Tom figured that the Cosywag probably didn't mean to be so harsh. Maybe he only spoke that way because he was scared. Tom resolved that whatever the reason for him being here, he would make the most of it and do all he could to help these lovable creatures.

The water was lapping gently along the shore and sparkling brightly in the sunlight. The sea seemed to change colour in the reflections of light dancing on the waves. It was the most beautiful sight Tom had ever seen.

All seventeen Cosywags stood with their furry feet touching the water with excited anticipation. The water lapped over their toes and caused a ripple of giggles down the line as they waited for the next command. A gentle breeze ruffled their fur and Tom had a feeling of exhilaration as he started the proceedings.

'Paws up all those who have had swimming lessons before,' he shouted.

Nobody moved. They all had pleading looks on their faces. They desperately wanted to discover again the delight of bathing in the inviting waters.

'Right!' Tom shouted in a commanding voice. 'Rule number one: Don't go out of your depth. Rule number two: Follow my instructions. Rule number three: Stay together. Rule number four: Don't fight the water. Rule number five ...'

Tom couldn't think of a rule for number five, so he said he'd tell them later if he thought of it.

Slowly, one by one, they stepped into the water. Some gave out gasps of delight and little giggles of embarrassment as their adventure to rediscover a lost art began. Tom watched with amusement as they paddled and explored the fresh water tickling their paws. He couldn't help thinking that this was all a bit too easy and something terrible was bound to happen sooner or later.

Suddenly the Cosywag on the end dived headlong into the water and disappeared from sight in a mass of bubbles and froth. Tom's heart seemed to leap into his mouth, and he waded as fast as he could to where the little Cosywag had disappeared. He plunged both hands deep into the water, swirling about and trying desperately to find the missing creature. Suddenly, about two metres away, a head bobbed up, and with a coughing and gurgling sound disappeared again just as quickly.

'Why don't they do as I ask?' mumbled Tom angrily, still groping about in the water.

With a great feeling of relief he found the terrified Cosywag and lifted him, dripping wet, out of the water.

Holding him up in front of him, Tom said, 'Don't you ever do that again! Follow my instructions!'

He waded back to the shore and placed him gently on the sand to recover. Then he turned to the other Cosywags who had been standing still like waxwork dummies, mesmerised by the scene before them.

'Still want to go through with this?' Tom asked.

'We want to save our land,' said Clarence. 'We must get to the place in the sea basin where the water is draining away. We have to find a way of filling in that hole and stopping the leak. In order to do that we must learn how to swim.'

'Very well,' said Tom. 'Let's carry on with the lesson, but don't anyone go out of their depth. The water can be dangerous, especially if you're inexperienced.'

Although there seemed to be nothing unusual about the sea, Tom wondered if there might be more surprises in store. He stretched up to his full height and looked out over the water. There was a disturbance in the currents some way out, but nothing that should concern them.

As the day wore on, the Cosywags progressed remarkably well in their swimming skills. They had a natural strength and agility that seemed out of all proportion to their soft cuddly appearance. They were strong and fast in the water, and Tom had a job to keep up with them, even with his favourite breast stroke. The day would have been an unqualified success, but for what happened next.

The Cosywags' confidence had been boosted no end by the ease with which they had picked up the techniques of swimming. They could not see the danger of over-confidence, and soon they made a fatal mistake. They swam further and further away from the shore, and closer and closer to the disturbance Tom had spotted earlier. It was a swirling whirlpool, and, almost in an act of defiance because of their new-found skills, the little Cosywags dared the suction of the waters to take them in its downward motion. The whirlpool was caused by the water leaking out of the plughole a hundred metres below the surface of the sea.

One by one they were irresistibly drawn into the swirling water. Tom saw what was about to happen and shouted for all he was worth.

'I've remembered rule number five! When you get into difficulty, don't panic!'

His words were lost in the roar of the waters. Round and round they went, downwards and anti-clockwise, losing control with every frightening turn. Down and down they went, heading straight for the hole in the seabed.

Without thinking, Tom thrashed at the water around him and, summoning every ounce of strength that he could, threw himself at the raging whirlpool, determined to rescue his friends. At the very last second before going under, he took in as much air as he could, then closed his mouth tightly as the crashing water threw his body into a downward spin.

He felt as though his lungs would pop like cheap party balloons, the pressure was so great. To his horror, he found that he was helpless against the tremendous force of the whirlpool, and had no choice but to await the certain doom of being sucked into the gaping black hole. His head thumped with rhythmic pain as his body was flung from side to side, knocking out of him any sense of direction.

Everything felt unreal, as if it was not really happening to him at all. Yet the deafening sound of the water, the pain he felt in his head and the way that his body was being thrown about were terrifyingly real enough!

His downward motion came to an abrupt and painful stop.

The little breath he had managed to retain in his lungs was violently punched away as he crashed into the metal grille covering the plughole. Water was rushing past his weakened and bruised body and down into the blackness of the hole. He tried desperately to move, but the pressure was too great. He knew he had only a few seconds to live.

It was difficult to be sure of anything in the rush of the water around him, but Tom thought he felt the grille suddenly jerk sideways. Instinctively he gripped one of the bars as tightly as he could; then everything went black.

There was no way of knowing how much time had gone by since his terrifying ordeal. He opened his eyes, thinking that he might be in heaven, and was surprised to find himself sitting inside a giant air bubble.

He was breathing normally, and he felt a vitality and freshness he had never felt before. Inside the bubble there was a beautiful fragrance like the smell of wild flowers in spring, and floating in the air there were tiny specks of silvery dust that transmitted tiny shafts of light in a million directions. Although he was in a strange place, Tom felt safe and secure, as if he could stay there for ever. He checked each part of his body in turn, moving each joint and exploring each muscle to see if there had been any damage. He wiggled his toes, then his feet, then his legs, arms, hands and fingers. Then, after bending from the waist a few times, he nodded his head backwards and forwards. He was grateful that the throbbing pain had gone.

It was then that he noticed faces pressed up against the outside wall of the transparent bubble, peering at him admiringly. He felt a bit silly when he realised that he had performed all those weird exercises in front of such a strange audience. Looking beyond the faces, which had taken on contorted shapes because of the pliable contours of the wall, he realised that he was still under the water and in fact was resting on the seabed. He also saw a violent disturbance in the sea not twenty metres away which he immediately recognised as the water rushing through the hole into oblivion.

To his surprise, three of the characters looking at him from outside the bubble were the Clawhammers he had seen earlier playing ball with that poor Cosywag.

He recognised Brutus, the one with the bad reputation, and wondered how they could survive under the water for so long without breathing. It was even more surprising when he counted at least twelve little furry animals with big blue eyes pressed up against the wall, with a mixture of sadness and relief in their expressions.

The Cosywags! They were safe! Tom could not identify Clarence, but he must be there somewhere. How could they too survive in the water with no air to breathe? It was difficult for him to take all this in. So much had happened so fast and nothing seemed to make any sense at all.

He was aware of words coming into his head, although he could hear nothing.

By the looks on the faces of the Cosywags, and the frantic gestures they were making with their paws, it was obvious they were trying to communicate something to him.

Following the instructions coming into his mind, he reached out and gently waved his hand through the silvery dust floating in the air, taking hold of as much of it as he could. He then took a deep breath and, throwing the dust to the side of the wall, got ready for the bubble to open and give him a way back to the surface of the Crystal Sea.

Very slowly and gracefully, the wall of the bubble where the dust had landed, folded back.

Tom expected an almighty rush of water, but the pressure and density of the curious air around him kept the water from the inside of the bubble. Tom, still holding his breath — rather unnecessarily as it happened — reached out his hand to touch the water. Then with one thrusting motion forward, he slid through the opening and into the sea, floating gently upwards until he reached the surface. He felt a strange sense of elation as he breathed in the cool air at last.

All around him little heads bobbed up and down. The Cosywags had come to escort him to the shore. He noticed that Brutus and the other two Clawhammers were already waiting for him at the water's edge.

Questions were tumbling into his mind in quick succession.

Who pulled him to safety from the brink of death down the black hole? What were the Clawhammers doing on the seabed? How could the Cosywags survive under the water for such a long time? What was the strange bubble that saved his life? And what exactly was the silvery dust that caused the bubble to open?

Why were there only twelve Cosywags escorting him back to the shore?

Where was his new friend, Clarence?

3

The Secret of the Crystal Sea

When Tom reached the shore he was surrounded by chattering Cosywags bubbling over with a mixture of excitement and bewildered sadness. Everyone was dripping wet, with hair and fur clinging to shivering bodies. Tom's clothes stuck to him like a second skin and he wished he had been able to bring his swimming trunks with him. Some big dry blankets were soon found, and his clothes were put out on the hot sand to dry in the afternoon sun while he wrapped one of the blankets around himself. The Cosywags were thrilled with their new-found swimming skills and the discovery that they could survive underwater.

The Jellybot was shaking all over with excitement while the Hummingbats watched with disapproving looks on their faces. They had not seen the Jellybot show emotion like this before. It seemed quite irregular and undignified to say the least! They were also concerned about his welfare. With the extra weight the Jellybot had accumulated owing to his lack of exercise, this kind of display would only put a strain on his heart which was already overworked.

There was an incredibly loud, high-pitched buzz coming from the Hummingbats as they hovered and fussed around the excited Jellybot, wings whizzing up and down, creating a blur of fluorescent blue. The air was certainly charged with emotion with all eyes darting at one moment to Tom, with a sense of gratitude and approval, and the next moment to the Jellybot, who was now beginning to make deep rumbling sounds as if he was about to break out in hilarious convulsions of laughter.

Brutus and his friends, still dripping wet, looked menacing as they stood in a little group with their aggressive and angry faces, like football fans after their team had been relegated to the fourth division.

There was another group of Clawhammers stomping up and down the shore line, holding a strange contraption which they passed over the beach in great sweeping motions. It looked like a cross between a metal detector and an upright carpet cleaner, with a tube leading into the huge bag that each Clawhammer wore on his back. It was a strange sight. Their large hammer-shaped heads, together with the slowly inflating bags made them look like hunchbacks that would topple over at any moment. Tom made an instant decision never to get too close to the strange creatures, for if one of them did fall over, anything underneath that head would almost certainly be hammered into the ground.

He stood on the beach near the sea with the warm blanket firmly wrapped around him, and every now and then would feel his feet engulfed by the water as it ebbed and flowed. Each time the water sank back under the next gently breaking wave, his bare feet sank a little into the soft golden sand.

Looking around him, he allowed his eyes to follow the contours of the land. There was an abundance of foliage round the shoreline, woven among the jagged rocks which sparkled in shades of blue, emerald green and gold. He wondered whether the rocks might be some form of crystal, hence giving their name to the Crystal Sea. The sheltered sandy beach stretched back to the high vertical cliff face beyond. All over the side of the cliff there were holes of all shapes and sizes ranging from tiny finger tip dimensions to a massive cave half way up the face.

There were no trees or bushes in the area — everything looked as though it should have been growing under the sea. The great tangled masses of green foliage had the appearance of seaweed. Some of it was dry and yellow round the edges and was clinging to the cliff face as if trying to escape from some prison-like existence.

Tom breathed in deeply. The air was cool and fresh and he felt an atmosphere of exhilaration tinged with a little sadness, as though all the beauty of nature and the inhabitants of this place were crying out for an ingredient missing from their lives.

'Who rescued me from the Black Hole?' asked Tom, suddenly becoming aware again of the commotion going on all around him.

'I did!' roared Brutus from across the beach.

Tom was flabbergasted! It was surely not possible that such an unfriendly creature would do such a thing. He stood in silence looking at Brutus who seemed to be standing ten feet tall.

'And those Cosywags had better keep their

promise, or else I will personally tear them limb from limb!' continued Brutus.

'That sounds more like the Brutus we know,' whispered Tom under his breath, hoping that the Clawhammers would not hear him.

'What was that you said?' shouted Brutus, determined not to let anything go without a challenge.

'Oh, nothing for you to be concerned about,' said Tom.

Tom thought he felt the ground shake as Brutus started stomping over towards him. He was definitely ten feet tall, and he looked almost as wide. The Jellybot suddenly stopped vibrating with laughter as he realised what was happening.

'Don't start anything you can't finish, Brutus,' he rumbled. 'Violence only shows an inner weakness.'

Tom thought that this was an extremely stupid thing to say, especially in the light of the fact that it was him Brutus was after, not the Jellybot! Nobody could match the power and physique of the Clawhammers, apart from the Jellybot, but then he was almost immobilised by the surrounding minefield.

Brutus seemed to know exactly what Tom was thinking. His massive head turned towards the Jellybot.

'Who do you think you are? What are you going to do about it? You're just a lump of useless flab! Any power you once had is gone and forgotten! You have no right to tell me what to do! I take my orders from one person alone!' Megagrit was the person Brutus was referring to, and that was whom the Clawhammers were in league with. How could the Clawhammers be so stupid as to be taken in by such a devious and wicked creature? Brutus continued stomping towards Tom.

Tom's feet were almost covered by the action of the water on the wet sand. He pulled his feet out one at a time and shuffled uneasily from side to side.

Brutus came within three metres of where Tom was standing, and suddenly there was a rush of tiny paws and a deafening buzzing sound as at least eight Cosywags and four of the Hummingbats made straight for Brutus. With the Hummingbats buzzing round his huge head making a deafening sound with their wings, and the Cosywags running round his feet at great speed, making high-pitched squealing noises, Brutus began to reel and rock all over the place. Tom automatically put his fingers in his ears to block out the head-splitting sounds in front of him. His feet seemed to be glued to the ground as he looked with utter amazement at the sight.

Brutus let out a frightening roar and began falling headlong to the ground, his great hammer head bearing down on Tom with deadly accuracy.

It was one of those vital, split-second reactions that saved the day, like a goalkeeper saving a penalty. Tom dived sideways, narrowly missing a large piece of jagged rock. The ground shook and Brutus' head sunk deeply into the sand where Tom had been standing. The other Clawhammers threw down their metal contraptions and came running over, kicking up sand and spray as they ran. Tom scrambled to his feet and joined the crowd gathered around Brutus.

There was no movement in that great body.

Tom had never taken a close look at a Clawhammer before. He never had any particular desire to do so. But now, at close quarters, he couldn't fail to notice the marks of corrosion all over the head of Brutus.

He looked around at the other Clawhammers. They all had the same corrosive marks on their heads. It was an unpleasant sight, as if some disease had attacked them and was slowly disfiguring their bodies like rust on metal.

'What's wrong with them?' he asked, with genuine concern in his voice.

'They've got Cankor disease,' said one of the Cosywags nearest to Tom. 'It's caused by exposure to the Crystal Sea coupled with extended periods of time in the desert places. The two ways don't mix and create this dreaded disease which eats the body away. Although the Clawhammers know all this, they refuse to get help from the one person who can cure them.'

'Who's that?' asked Tom.

'The Rainchild,' they said.

Tom remembered the Jellybot mentioning that name when he was explaining to him how the land of Crystalan was under threat from the wicked Megagrit. This evil character obviously wanted to take control by persuading everybody to break free from the rule of the Rainchild.

'Is Brutus dead?' asked the Jellybot.

'No,' said one of the other Clawhammers gruffly, 'but the disease has weakened him, and it takes time for him to recover after a fall like that. He was already weak after his desperate struggle to save you, Tom.'

'I still don't know what happened down there,' said Tom, with exasperation.

The Cosywags all started talking at once.

'Hang on a minute! One at a time,' said Tom.

The air seemed to take on an unusual chill and Tom noticed that the sun was beginning to get very low in the sky out over the sea. Interesting colours began shooting off the surface of the sea as the angle of the sun's rays changed moment by moment. The huddle of creatures on the beach seemed to grow in size and shape as the failing light played tricks on the eyes.

One of the Cosywags, Clarissa, took up the story.

'We ventured too close to the whirlpool during our swimming lesson. You see, our ancestors all had the ability to live under the water as well as on the land. Their bodies were wonderfully designed with special breathing apparatus to enable them to do that. We have never ventured into the water in our lifetime, because we've grown used to living on the land, and although there were stories of Cosywags living in the sea, we never believed them.'

Another Cosywag put his paw round her shoulder and continued the account.

'When the whirlpool took us and we knew we were headed towards the Black Hole and certain death, we were forced into re-activating our underwater biological functions. We should not have been surprised when we discovered that all we had heard from our ancestors was true. Most of us managed to cling on to the bars of the grid, although our beloved Clarence and four of our close friends were not so lucky, and slipped through the bars into the blackness.'

Some of the Cosywags started quietly crying, with big tears rolling out of their big blue eyes. They began hugging one another and looked forlorn and dejected. A lump came into Tom's throat as he remembered the first time he met Clarence after being rescued from the minefield.

Clarissa continued. 'With our new-found strength

33

in the water, we were able to break away from the grid and were immediately confronted by three Clawhammers, one of whom was Brutus. Some of their comrades had stolen the Purple Plug and they were left behind to guard the Black Hole to ensure the water would drain away. When, to our horror, we saw you pinned to the grid, we pleaded with Brutus to help you. We had to make a promise to him before he would act.'

'What promise?' asked Tom.

'Something we have to do that we will find very difficult.'

Tom didn't ask what this was. He knew they would tell him when they were ready. He was eager to hear the rest of the story.

'When they stole the Purple Plug, they had to cut it free from the chain that attached it to the grid. Part of the chain had been left behind and was still attached. With his superior strength, Brutus was able to pull you away safely, together with the grid, by using the chain. We used some of the silvery freedom dust to open the bubble so that you could get the life-giving air you need. You know the rest of the story.'

By now, Brutus had managed to get up from his face-down position and was leaning up against a rock surrounded by his comrades. There was a large round hole where his head had hit the ground. He looked sad and tired, his pride hurt, and the growing discomfort of the Cankor disease was obviously worrying him.

There were mixed emotions floating around in Tom's mind. Although he was glad to be alive, he could not understand why the Clawhammers were being so obstinate in refusing help for their disease and why they had stolen the Purple Plug for Megagrit in the first place.

He could resist it no longer. He walked up to where Brutus was seated, and looked him square in the eye.

'Why? Why did you do it?'

'You aggravated me,' grunted Brutus.

'No, I didn't mean that,' said Tom. 'I want to know why you are betraying the creatures in your world and why you are rebelling against the Rainchild. From all I've heard, he wants the best for all of you. It just doesn't make sense.'

'How can there be a Rainchild when he allows such diseases to attack us?' said Brutus aggressively. 'For all I know he may only exist in the imagination of these creatures. I know Megagrit exists for he has offered us a miraculous cure.'

'But at what price?' asked Tom, already knowing the answer.

'We are co-operating with him in the restoration of our world. The old ways are extinct, we must look to the future and a new way of life. Even now the rest of my comrades are marching to Megagrit's secret castle with the Purple Plug. Megagrit has promised to save us when he has it in his possession.'

'If you believe that, you'll believe anything,' sneered Tom.

'That's the trouble,' said Clarissa, joining in the conversation, 'they are so gullible, they would believe anything.'

'Yes, even when the answer is staring them in the face,' concluded the Jellybot, his deep penetrating voice wafting across the beach to where they stood.

The sun had almost disappeared into the sea now and the sky was ablaze with fantastic colours of red and mauve, forming a canvas for another unique sunset.

Brutus, now fully recovered, was stomping back with his comrades to the clearing on the beach where they had been working.

'What are they up to now?' questioned Tom.

It was the Jellybot who answered.

'They are collecting the silvery freedom dust in their sacks using their dust detectors. It is made by a special process at the bottom of the sea, and is carried by the current to the shore. The water is full of it, but it is hard to collect in any other way. They are taking sackfuls of it to Megagrit.'

Tom thought that they must have been very serious about getting the dust, for it was rapidly getting colder and darker and they were still working frantically up and down the edge of the beach. They were like shadows grappling for survival before darkness comes.

Conscious that he seemed to have spent all his time asking questions since he had been in this strange world, Tom almost didn't ask — but in the end he couldn't resist it. He weaved his way through the minefield towards the Jellybot, a line of Cosywags following on behind him. He called out as he got nearer.

'Can I ask one more question?'

'One more;' said the Jellybot.

'What does the silvery freedom dust do?'

'You have already seen something of what it can do when it released you from inside the bubble. But it has far greater, more valuable properties.'

All the creatures were slowly gathering round the Jellybot, where they always had a sense of strength and security, to hear again what they already knew but found hard to believe.

'The dust,' he continued, 'has a releasing quality. When in the waters of the Crystal Sea it brings life and liberty to all those who take it in. However, when you benefit from the unique qualities of this gift, you must also accept the responsibility that goes with it. You must learn how to use your freedom wisely and in a way that fulfils the purposes of the Rainchild. This is true freedom.'

A sad look came over the Jellybot's face.

'However, when in the hands of evil, personal freedom is used as an excuse to do whatever is desired and because of these selfish aims, it can only bring destruction, heartbreak and death upon others.'

'But they are giving it to Megagrit!' Tom blurted out in horror.

'Exactly,' said the Jellybot.

It was now almost completely dark.

4

The Burning of the Gusters

After sleeping for at least eight hours, Tom was woken up by the wailing sound he had heard shortly after he arrived in this strange world. The sand beneath him vibrated at the resonance of the sound, and the attractive sweet smell of the Jellybot brought his mind back into focus as he remembered the serious words of the night before.

The familiar sound was coming from the Jellybot whose eyes were half closed. His mouth was now shaped like a car tyre, and he was obviously in a state of deep concentration and involved in some serious business.

Tom wondered how the creature could shape his lips in such a perfect circle and began trying to do the same, pulling his mouth into unnatural shapes that made him look like a demented goldfish.

'Is that some kind of face exercise you are doing?' enquired Clarissa with interest.

'Oh no!' said Tom, with amusement. 'I was just trying to copy the Jellybot. That certainly is a funny face he's making this morning! What is he doing anyway?'

'He's sending out a homing signal for the Gusters,' answered Clarissa. 'We are expecting them to arrive any day now after their hazardous journey.'

Seeing the puzzled look on Tom's face and realising how confusing all this must be to him, she started to explain in more detail.

'The Gusters are the craft that carry our people across the Crystal Sea.' She looked reflective for a moment, and then, shrugging her shoulders, looked out over the gently moving waves.

'What are you thinking about?' asked Tom.

'I was wondering why, for so many generations, we have ignored the sacred writings of our ancestors. If we had believed them, we would never have needed the Gusters in the first place. We all have the ability to live and move under the water, but we have created these huge cumbersome boats that are a waste of time and effort. It's funny how quickly you can forget the wise ways of the past.'

Tom felt the warmth of the sun on his face as the early morning heat began to drive the yellowy mist away. The mist formed during the night, like a suspended cloud obscuring the beauty of the bay. He noticed a large number of the Cosywags standing on the beach looking out to sea. Some were perched on top of the jagged crystal rocks in quite a dangerous fashion, trying to get a better view. They could easily have slipped on the foliage which was draped in a haphazard fashion in every nook and cranny. It wasn't looking so green now, but was getting slightly brown round the edges.

Some of the Cosywags were slowly walking up and down looking at the sand, and every now and then they would glance out to sea with worried expressions on their faces.

'A watched pot never boils!' said Tom, pulling on his dry clothes.

As soon as he had said it, he wished he hadn't. It was one of those ridiculous sayings people always quoted at the most inappropriate times, making the situation seem ten times worse than it really was.

The Cosywags were obviously concerned for the safe return of their friends, travelling in the Gusters.

Clarissa nudged him on the shoulder. 'Here,' she said, 'I have some food for you.'

It was only then that he realised how hungry he was. He hadn't eaten for twenty-four hours and was famished. 'Wow! Thank you very much!' said Tom, looking at the small tray of food before him.

He didn't recognise the things he was eating, but they tasted delicious; the sweet and savoury smells wafted into his nostrils, making his mouth water with anticipation at every bite. There was a square plate full of a thick white substance which looked like mousse, but when he put it in his mouth, it felt as if a taste explosion had been detonated on the back of his tongue. It reminded him of his favourite sweets, known as Fizz Whizz, and sold in small packets down at the local newsagents. In a round bowl with a handle on each side, there was some hot green liquid. Apparently this was extracted from the green plants around the sea shore and used as a refreshing and healthy drink. Then there were some transparent round vegetables that looked like marbles — and their texture was similar, too.

'Be careful you don't get those stuck in your throat,' warned Clarissa, pointing at them. 'They are extremely good for you, but you must suck them slowly and don't try to swallow them whole!'

She was beginning to sound like his mum.

Suddenly loud excited noises came from the beach. Tom jumped up and looked out to sea. There on the horizon were at least six boats. It was difficult to tell from this distance, but they seemed to be triangular, with one angle pointing forward as the prow. They were obviously very stable because the waves, which were quite fierce further out, were having little or no effect on their progress. Shafts of light from the sun reflected on the walls of the boats, making them look like three-sided mirrors.

Two thirds of the way up the triangular sides was a single line of windows, and as they got nearer to the shore you could clearly see their precious cargo. There must have been at least a hundred Cosywags on those boats, all eager to reach the shore. The deep, smooth whirring sound of powerful engines, which were relentlessly pushing the vessels through the sea, got louder as they approached.

It was a magnificent sight. Groups of Cosywags lined the beach, waving chains of beautiful white water flowers gathered especially from the rock pools around the edges of the bay. Bright red and gold flags were strung up at every available fixing point and flapped in uncontrollable abandon as the breeze caught them from all directions, as if even nature was joining in the excitement of the moment. This was the traditional Cosywag welcome to family and friends returning home.

Without warning, there was a fierce whooshing sound. Great rocks and stones shot over the heads of the waiting crowd and out towards the Gusters. There were great splashes as the missiles landed around the helpless boats. One large rock caused what looked like a lightning flash as it ricocheted off the side of one of them.

'We're under attack!' shouted Clarissa. 'Take cover!'

Taken completely by surprise, Tom was knocked violently sideways as a huge lump of hard mud struck him just over his right ear. Panic broke out and the frightened Cosywags on the shore ran in all directions, the white flowers falling to the ground. Some lay wounded on the sand as a hail of stones came down from the top of the high cliffs behind them. The Jellybot let out a shriek of pain when a boulder landed in the middle of his back.

Tom scrambled to his feet, grabbed Clarissa and ran as fast as he could towards the cliff face. He was hoping against hope that he would put his feet in the right places, avoiding the deadly minefield around the Jellybot. He had walked the pathway several times now, but travelling at a sprint with a frightened Cosywag in his arms and rocks whistling past his ears didn't exactly help.

Out of breath and puffing uncontrollably, Tom collapsed in a heap at the base of the cliff. Both he and Clarissa were safe for the time being. Whatever, or whoever was up there doing this terrible thing, deserved to be punished! How dare they attack the poor defenceless Jellybot and all his Cosywag companions!

Tom noticed that there were no Clawhammers around, but he could not believe they would sink so low as to do this. In any case, it wasn't their style. They preferred face-to-face confrontation, not attacks from behind.

Two Hummingbats sent sand spraying everywhere as they swooped in to land next to Tom and Clarissa. They spoke in urgent whispers to Clarissa who then passed on the news of their discovery to Tom.

'There are three Sandmen on the top of the cliff and they have a big machine which they are using to catapult the rocks at us and our friends out there on the sea. They are the wicked soldiers of Megagrit: he wants to destroy us so that he can have the silvery freedom dust all to himself. As if he hasn't already done enough damage by stealing the Purple Plug! Now he wants to kill us as well!'

The hail of stones and rocks continued to rain down on the beach, and other larger missiles were being catapulted out to sea, many of them hitting their targets. There were explosions all around as the rocks hit the metal spikes of the minefield. Tom felt angry and helpless in the face of such mindless destruction.

Then an idea came to him. He was surprised that he could even think of being so brave and bold, yet he knew something had to be done before it was too late.

'Get as many of the Cosywags over to the cliff face as you can,' he said to Clarissa and the two Hummingbats who seemed to be waiting for orders. 'It's the most sheltered place on the beach.'

'What about the Jellybot?' cried Clarissa.

'There's nothing we can do to help him,' shouted Tom. 'Be careful where you tread; there are still a lot of mines lying around that could go up at any minute. Just answer me one question.'

'What's that?' called Clarissa, trying to make herself heard through the noise.

'Is there any way to get up there without having to climb the cliff face?'

'No, there isn't,' she said. 'The cliffs surround us on three sides. The only way out from here is into the sea.'

'Right. Do as I asked. I'll see you later,' shouted Tom.

'But, you're not going to ...' Clarissa's voice faded into disbelieving horror as Tom started searching for a foothold in the cliff edge.

'Don't try to stop me,' said Tom, suddenly feeling very grown up. 'I've got to do this.'

Clarissa couldn't bear to look. She ran off in search of her injured friends, and Tom started the long, dangerous climb to the top.

There were plenty of holes in the cliff face, as Tom had observed the day before, but the difficulty was finding the ones that were firm enough to hold his weight. Once he had managed to climb to about three or four metres he felt fairly certain that he could reach the top. He was very good at climbing trees back home and although this was a little different, the confidence in knowing where to put his feet and the sheer instinct of self preservation kept him to the task at hand. Although most of the beach was bathed in sunlight, the cliff face and the beach at the base of the cliff were still in the shade. The sun would soon be high in the sky and its light would break over the top of the cliff, revealing clearly the hard personal struggle going on part-way up the side.

He paused for a moment and looked at the scene around him. The devastation was frightening.

There were potholes all over the beach, made either by exploding mines or by the impact of the falling rocks. Hundreds of the white flowers had been trampled into the ground and the colourful flags hung helplessly in weird, broken formations. Clarissa was doing a great job getting the Cosywags to safety, but Tom couldn't help noticing that some were definitely beyond help. The poor Jellybot was almost totally buried in a mass of rocks and gravel. Had they lost him and his wonderful, friendly personality for ever?

Tom then turned his attention to the sea, and could hardly bear to look.

There was smoke streaming from the windows of one of the Gusters, and little Cosywags were jumping frantically into the sea. He wondered whether they realised that they had a natural affinity for the water and could swim easily if only they tried. Another of the Gusters was drifting dangerously near to the whirlpool, and although they were obviously very stable boats, it would not be able to withstand the downward pull of that water.

With a new determination, Tom continued his slow progress to the top. The cliff was almost vertical in places, and his hands were getting sore as he gripped the crumbling rock. He was suddenly dazzled by a shaft of light as the sun's rays lit up the side of the cliff. Momentarily blinded, he paused, hanging on to a piece of solid rock. He would have to double his efforts if he was going to reach the top unnoticed by the enemy.

Without warning a lump of mud came whizzing down towards him from one of the Sandmen peering over the side. They had obviously become aware of his presence, and this made him feel even more vulnerable and helpless.

He clung desperately to the side, willing his muscles to take the strain. If one of those rocks hit him he would surely fall to his death. He leaned out as much as he dared and noticed that about one-and-a-half metres above him there was a very large hole, like the entrance to a cave. It must have been halfway up the cliff face. If he could just get to that point and haul himself in, it would give him time to rest and think.

Just as he felt there was a glimmer of hope, a piece of jagged rock hurtled past him, ripping his shirt as easily as a razor blade cutting through tissue paper. It sent him completely off balance and he found himself hanging by one hand and desperately trying to find another foothold to steady his swinging body.

Fortunately the Hummingbats were at hand.

Tom did not mind in the least the deafening buzzing sound of those tiny wings, when he realised that they had swung their golden rope firmly round his aching body, and in spite of being bombarded from above they were lifting him the short distance to the cave entrance.

He lay there panting for a few moments, then hearing the cries of the Cosywags below, got to his feet and quickly felt his way along the wall of the cave. He noticed a welcome glimmer of light in the darkness, and as he moved further into the cave, the light became bigger and brighter.

He stopped suddenly in his tracks as he noticed some drawings cut into the wall of the cave. The light made them look lifelike as it shimmered across the surface of the rock.

Then he saw it. The most beautiful picture he had ever seen.

It was of a young boy, probably no older than he was, with a strong handsome face and a golden cloak over his shoulders. He was standing on a golden cloud surrounded by sunlight. Underneath the cloud there were big raindrops reflecting all the colours of the rainbow as they fell to earth.

Tom gasped. He knew who it was, but he dared not say it, even to himself.

He stood in silence for a few moments. Then, when he had collected his thoughts, he turned quickly in the direction of the light and made his way out through a hole, not more than a metre wide, into the open. He was standing on top of the cliff and looking out over a vast expanse of white, flat land. In the distance he could clearly see a desert stretching back to the horizon.

Suddenly aware of noises behind him, he swung round and saw three ugly creatures, shaped like rugby balls, only many times bigger — at least the size of a minibus. They had stumpy little arms and legs attached to bodies that appeared to be made of sand. There were blemishes and blotches all over them where dirt, grit and grime had stuck to them. Tom watched them manoeuvring their great bodies backwards and forwards in a kind of rolling motion. Two of them were busy loading their firing machine and the other one was haphazardly throwing anything he could lay his hands on, down onto the beach below.

They had not noticed Tom watching them from behind, so realising his advantage, he quickly sprang into action.

He charged towards the biggest one, just as he was about to throw a large lump of mud down onto the beach. For a moment he felt as if he had hit a brick wall. There seemed to be no movement in that unwieldy body. But gradually, almost unnoticeably, the huge bulk began to roll towards the edge of the cliff. Tom carried on pushing with every ounce of energy he could muster. There was a sudden yell, and the Sandman went crashing down onto the beach, smashing into pieces as he landed. Tom almost went over the edge with him, but managed to get to his feet just as another Sandman, with a violent and angry expression on his face, came rolling towards him, gathering speed with every metre.

Tom waited until the very last moment, then diving out of the way, sent the second Sandman crashing to his death.

The third Sandman did not wait around: he made his escape as fast as he could down into the white land, heading for the desert and his master, the evil Megagrit.

Now that the danger had passed, the Hummingbats lifted Tom with their golden rope, and a great cheer came up from all the Cosywags as they lowered him to the beach once more.

No sound came from the Jellybot.

Tom and Clarissa stood in the middle of the beach and surveyed the scene. Some lives had been lost. One of the Gusters had been taken by the whirlpool to the bottom of the ocean. Another was on fire, drifting aimlessly in the open sea. Four of the Gusters had survived the ordeal and were rapidly approaching the landing bay.

There was great excitement as families were reunited and suddenly the beach came alive in a hubbub of sounds. Voices rose emotionally as loved ones embraced one another. Some were sharing their shock and sadness at having lost friends and family members. They had come through a highly dangerous encounter and they all knew that the battle had only just begun.

There was a lot of activity going on. Provisions were being unloaded from the Gusters, stories of adventures across the sea were being shared, the cleaning-up operation was fully under way and there were Cosywags all over the Jellybot, clearing away the debris that had almost buried him alive.

A great cheer echoed across the beach as the Jellybot began to move. He was very shaken, but apart from a few bruises he was fine. Tom climbed up onto his nose, in the same position he had been in when he entered Crystalan in such an unruly manner. While a few of the Cosywags cleaned him up as best they could, Tom carefully extracted bits of grit from his eyes.

'Stop blinking,' said Tom, with a hint of relief in his voice. 'How am I supposed to get this gunge out of your eyes, when you keep fidgeting about?'

'I can't help it,' said the Jellybot, grateful to be alive, but a little uncomfortable at this necessary operation.

Suddenly every eye was on the last Guster to make the landing. The door slowly opened, and out stepped the beautiful Princess Amathena. Tom nearly fell right off the nose of the Jellybot. Her beauty was breathtaking.

The Jellybot couldn't resist a comment. 'Love at first sight?' he said mischievously, looking straight at Tom.

'I think you could be right,' Tom replied with a tremble in his voice.

There was much sadness that night, as everyone gathered in small groups around the warm glow of bonfires on the beach, comforting and consoling the bereaved. Torches were ignited one by one to give more light, as the evening drew on. They all knew that life could never be the same again.

Among the many friends who had arrived in the

Gusters were Clive and Claude, the two brothers of Clarence. They were devastated when they heard of his death.

The Princess Amathena told of her disappointment; how she had travelled across the Crystal Sea with the Cosywags in search of the Purple Plug, and how they had watched the Clawhammer procession, carrying the Plug on their backs out across the salt flats and into the desert on their way to Megagrit. She spoke of her sadness and disbelief at their futile actions. Now they had returned to the Jellybot dejected and defeated, their hopes smashed, their future gone. There was nothing they could do now to stop the sea draining away and the final destruction of their world.

Tom didn't think he had any right to speak in the presence of someone so important, but he had to say it.

'You must do two things,' he said confidently.

Everyone looked at him, rather startled that he dared to speak in this way in front of a princess, but he was not deterred by their disapproving looks.

'One,' he continued, 'you must burn the remaining Gusters as an act of faith. If you really believe in what your ancient writings declare, then you should act on it now. You don't need the boats. Many of you have already proved that. You have been given the ability to live and move under water.'

He paused for a reaction. No one said a word, so he continued with greater urgency in his voice.

'Secondly, you must trust the Rainchild.'

'But how do we know he will help? How do we know he even exists?' said Clive.

'I know,' said Tom, 'I've seen him.'

'Where?' asked Clarissa with bated breath.

'In the cave on the cliff face,' said Tom with a big smile on his face.

It was an eerie sight.

They all sat around Princess Amathena looking out to sea. The Gusters cast black silhouettes against the crimson background of the setting sun. Then flames began to engulf each boat one by one and slowly, with dignity, they disappeared under the sea. Columns of smoke spiralled towards the sky.

The deed was done.

The real adventure was about to begin!

5
The Treachery of Megagrit

He raised his thick stumpy arm high over his head, took careful aim, and with a fast whiplash motion, sent a huge lump of mud and grit hurtling towards the terrified Sandman.

The long dark corridors of the castle of Megagrit, deep in the heart of the desert, resounded to the hysterical shrieks and screaming abuse of its master as he towered above the unfortunate creature before him.

'How dare you return as a failure into my presence! You will pay with your life!'

The Sandman, arriving back from the partially successful attack mission on the Cosywags, tried to make his excuses, stammering and faltering as he went. He knew his end was near. Quickly turning and rolling towards the thick stone doors, he tried to make his escape from the wrath of Megagrit, but before he could get more than three metres, another cruel missile struck him in the middle of the back, and his weakened body could take no more.

'Get rid of that useless pile of sand!' shouted Megagrit at two Sandman guards by the door.

'Immediately, Your Megagrit,' they said respectfully, and rolled over quickly to where the body lay.

'Learn from this!' snarled Megagrit. 'Let no one in my kingdom run away from a battle!'

'Yes, Your Megagrit,' replied the Sandmen, dragging their comrade out of the huge audience room through the heavy stone doors.

The booming sound of the doors closing echoed around the cavernous, windowless room which was dimly lit by flaming torches hanging at intervals round the dirty, thick sand walls. The large expanse of smooth stone floor was littered with lumps of dirt and grit resulting from other cruel attacks from Megagrit on his defenceless soldiers.

It was hard to imagine how anyone could serve such a tyrant as Megagrit, yet the Sandmen had remained loyal under his regime for many years. They would do anything he commanded, partly out of fear and partly out of a strange kind of attraction to his evil brand of power. They had built the imposing castle out of the desert with their own bare hands and there was even a legend sometimes talked about among the people of Crystalan, that many of them gave their bodies as a sacrifice in order to become strengthening buttresses for the walls of the castle. It was claimed that if you looked carefully, you could sometimes detect the large round shapes of what once were living beings in the very fabric of the walls themselves. Such was the hold of Megagrit on his people. But he was not content with that — his desire was to take over the land of Crystalan completely.

There he was, sitting on a throne made of large

stone slabs. At regular intervals he would push his arm into a large round stone cauldron at his side and stir the thick mixture of mud, grit, stones, tar and nail clippings. He spread more layers of it around his already bulbous body, making him look even more grotesque. He was almost as tall as a double-decker bus, and the bulges all over his large oval body looked like outsize festering boils about to break out. When he was angry, which was most of the time, his eyes seemed to treble in size, sticking out like footballs from his swollen face. Even though he was bulky and had short stumpy arms and legs, he was surprisingly agile.

'When I have the silvery freedom dust, I will put it in the cauldron and it too will become part of my body, giving me unlimited power!' he shrieked.

Nobody was listening.

The procession of Clawhammers carrying the Purple Plug was now only three hours away from the Castle of Megagrit. There was no sound to be heard apart from the steady rhythmic plod of determined feet. The hot sand burned them with every step and the glaring reflections bouncing off the tiny particles dazzled them, causing them to peer ahead through half closed eyes. Many of them were suffering seriously from the effects of the Cankor disease which afflicted them and they were getting weaker by the hour. What kept them going was the thought that they would soon receive their reward for delivering the Purple Plug. Megagrit would give them the cure for their dreaded disease, and then they could really begin to live again.

Six of the Clawhammers bowed low under the weight of the large round Plug. It was three metres from side to side and about half a metre thick. Nobody knew what material it was made from, but the purple haze emanating from its surface gave it a regal appearance.

The considerable strength of the Clawhammers had already kept them going for six gruelling hours in the hot desert sun. Apart from those carrying the Plug, there were twelve more of them, laden with bags full of the silvery freedom dust that had been collected on the shores of the Crystal Sea. Several others carried containers full of the water which was an absolute necessity for their survival. After every hour, they would stop marching and each take a carefully measured portion of the water.

As they plodded over a long sloping sand dune, the castle slowly came into view in the distance. Rising up out of the desert it was imposing and frightening. It looked unreal, like a fragile sand-castle on the sea shore, and yet the closer they got, the more formidable and ugly it looked. Its battlements reached up like defiant children challenging authority. On each of the four corners, high towers stood like silent guardsmen.

Suddenly, from the direction of the castle, at least twenty Sandmen came rolling towards the Clawhammers, who stopped and waited for the welcoming party to reach them. Yet the welcome was far from courteous: the Sandmen's manner was abrupt.

'Megagrit has sent us to escort you the rest of the way to the castle. Do exactly as you are told or you will face the consequences!'

The Clawhammers were not used to being spoken to like that, but they had no choice but to comply with the instructions. They had a strange, uneasy feeling as they marched into the courtyard of the castle and carefully lowered the Purple Plug to the ground.

'Don't put it there,' yelled Megagrit, from a double window in the main building in front of them, 'Bring it here to me!'

They picked up the Plug and carried it with some difficulty up the stone steps and into the building. As the large stone door swung back, they saw Megagrit sitting on a raised platform at the far end of the large audience room. On one side of him was his stone cauldron, and on each edge of the platform a gigantic torch burned brightly with flames leaping angrily into the air.

'Bring it closer,' he growled, 'and give me the freedom dust!'

Bruno, one of the Clawhammers, stepped forward as the spokesman for the rest.

'Megagrit, we have fulfilled our side of the bargain. Now it is your turn. We need the cure for our disease before our comrades begin to die.'

Megagrit rose slowly on his stumpy legs. 'How dare you address me in that way!' he shouted in his gravelly voice. 'It's "*YOUR* Megagrit". I am a superior being and I should be addressed as such. Show some respect. After all, you are depending on me for your lives!'

Under normal circumstances the Clawhammers would never have submitted themselves to such an unpleasant creature, but they had to find the cure for the Cankor disease.

'Your Megagrit,' said Bruno slowly and deliberately, 'we will give you our honour and respect when you keep your promise to us.'

'Not so fast,' replied Megagrit deviously, 'we have

another common interest to be sorted out. The destruction of the Rainchild.'

The tone of his voice sent a chill up the back of all those present. It had a terrible, evil whine to it.

'After all, you want to be free, don't you? You want to build a new life free from the domination of the waters of the Crystal Sea? Get me the Rainchild and all will be well!'

'He has done us no harm,' said Bruno, 'and we have kept to the terms of our agreement. Now keep your promise.'

One of the Clawhammers suddenly collapsed on the floor groaning with pain. The container he was carrying fell to the floor and a trickle of water ran across the floor towards the platform.

'Get that away from me!' screamed Megagrit, with a hint of fear in his voice, 'You'll pay for this attack on my person!'

He turned, and with an amazing agility, disappeared down behind the platform into an adjoining room.

The Clawhammers gathered around their fallen comrade, but it was too late. The fatigue of the long journey coupled with the progress of the disease had taken its toll.

They were surrounded by Sandmen, some of whom dragged the body of their comrade out of sight, while others ushered them out of the audience room and down a long tube-like corridor. Their captors seemed to be allergic to water, for they all avoided getting too close to the remaining container, carried by one of their comrades who walked rather unsteadily at the back. It was difficult for them to walk on the curved floor surface, but the Sandmen rolled quickly and efficiently along, the contours of their body fitting exactly into the shape of the floor.

The Clawhammers were shown to a large windowless dormitory and the door was locked. The room was obviously designed as sleeping quarters for the Sandmen, for the beds were round shaped indentations in the floor, in which they could sit and sleep without fear of rolling away. The only light came from one flaming torch in the corner and there was an irritating dry acrid smell hovering in the thin air. They wondered what they had let themselves in for. If Megagrit would not keep his promise, they would have to use force to obtain the cure.

They huddled together to make their plans.

Sandmen, and even Megagrit himself, seemed so strong and arrogant on the outside, and yet they appeared to be very vulnerable in certain situations. The Clawhammers were confident that in hand-to-hand combat, there would be no contest! Their superior strength and physical fitness bore no comparison to the sluggish and bulky bodies of the Sandmen. Their one glaring disadvantage was that the Cankor disease had advanced so rapidly in some of them that paralysis had begun to set in, and they were not as agile as they once had been.

Bruno looked around at his companions. He wondered how his brother, Brutus, was getting on, guarding the Black Hole from any possible intruders. He had a nagging feeling that a terrible mistake had been made. But they had come too far to go back now.

'Let's get out of this prison and search the castle. We must find our cure before it is too late,' he commanded. 'We still have enough strength left to knock down these flimsy walls. We won't be double-crossed by an ugly lump of grit!'

That got them all moving.

They stood in line, one behind the other, facing the flat sand wall next to the stone doorway. If they could penetrate this by using their massive hammer heads, there would be no need to break the lock on the door. They could simply walk through a hole in the wall!

They eagerly waited their turn; one by one, each fell with his whole weight on to the dormitory wall. Apart from a dull thumping sound made by the impact there was not much noise. But every attempt to break down the wall inflicted acute pain on the Clawhammers because their heads were already sore from the disease. As each one struck the wall, his companions would help him back on his feet to the end of the line to wait for his next hit.

Bruno felt proud to have friends with such courage and determination. Every blow cost them dearly.

Slowly but surely the wall began to split and fall away. The hammering continued, until at last a small hole led into the corridor beyond.

'Stop!' shouted Bruno.

His friends collapsed in a heap of tired, sore bodies, waiting for the next command.

'We must be very careful at this point that we don't bring the roof down on our heads. We nearly have a way through, but take it gently from now on.'

The sleeping guards in the dormitory next door were suddenly aroused by the banging as the Clawhammers continued their attack on the wall. Rolling out of their beds and into the tubeway corridor, the Sandmen headed quickly in the direction of the sound. The Clawhammers did not notice the rumbling noise of their approach because they were concentrating intensely on the job in hand.

As the first Clawhammer crawled through the gaping hole in the wall, a Sandman, travelling at speed down the corridor, rolled straight over him and pushed him mercilessly into the ground. Undeterred, two more Clawhammers crawled through the hole and stepped into the corridor. They moved as quickly as their failing bodies would allow, in the direction of the audience room where they had first met the evil Megagrit.

Two more Sandmen were rapidly gaining on them as they gathered speed down the winding corridors. Realising they could not possibly reach a safe position without being overcome by the approaching guards, the two Clawhammers turned to face their opponents, and leaning forwards with their hammer heads at the ready, waited for the inevitable impact.

The Sandmen saw what was about to happen.

Sand, grit and smoke poured out from underneath them as they tried frantically to stop their rapid progress to destruction. Their efforts were in vain, as, with an almighty collision, the hammer heads sunk deeply into the brittle sand bodies of the guards. There was a domino effect as several other guards ploughed into the back of the leading one. The huge weight of this multi-bodied pile up was a terrific strain on the two Clawhammers, and they staggered backwards in a stupefied daze towards the audience room a few metres beyond.

They fell into the large room and were confronted by the towering figure of Megagrit, who, with one whiplash of his stumpy arm, sent a deadly missile of rock and grit hurtling towards them.

They were never to see their beloved home again.

Back in the dormitory, Bruno was horrified at what was happening. 'Make the hole bigger, it's all or nothing,' he cried.

The remaining Clawhammers drove their bodies hard against the wall and with a great crash, the wall collapsed and the roof fell in on top of them, burying them in grit, sand and mud.

For a moment, nothing stirred.

By now the sun had gone down, although they had not realised it, for there were very few windows in this fortress. The torch was still standing, its flames licking the cold night air and creating weird shadows on the pile of debris.

Bruno was the first to move. He managed to push aside the heavy weight of rock on his back, and emerged, bruised but alive, into the open. He quickly dug with his claw-like hands into the mound before him.

It was only a matter of minutes, yet to Bruno, it seemed like hours, digging desperately to recover his courageous friends. Gradually the offending pile of broken wall and roof was pushed to one side, and the Clawhammers hugged one another, glad to be alive. It was highly unusual for Clawhammers to show emotion, but the occasion seemed to demand it.

They scrambled over the fallen debris, determined to make their escape. They would return to the wicked Megagrit in large numbers and make sure he would never break a promise again.

Jumping over the remaining bits of wall that were still standing, they made their way quickly out into the night — then they were suddenly stopped in their tracks.

All around them fiery torches sparked into life, lighting up the night sky. There in the middle stood the terrifying figure of Megagrit, casting strangely deformed shadows that seemed to jump wildly in all directions as the flames flickered.

'You didn't think you could win, did you?' he said calmly.

Bruno looked behind him at the pile of rubble that used to be a dormitory and in the light of the flames, spotted an overturned container. The last drops of water were trickling out onto the ground. There was a clearly defined channel cut out by the flow of the water, and every grain of sand and grit that had come into contact with it had completely disintegrated.

'Of course,' Bruno muttered, 'the waters of the Crystal Sea hold the key to victory and freedom. Why didn't we see it earlier?'

'Too late!' screamed Megagrit. 'You lose!'

6

The Arrival of the Slickwingers

There was a noticeable drop in the level of the water around the beach as more and more jagged crystal rocks began appearing above the waterline. They all had masses of green weed draped over them in different patterns as if they were in a fashion parade. The foliage further up the beach was now almost totally brown through lack of the precious water, and if you passed within three metres of them, the smell was rather unpleasant to say the least!

Once again the whole bay was alive with activity.

A line of Cosywags stretched from the shoreline all the way up to where the Jellybot lay motionless and still. They passed containers of the refreshing water one to the other, the last one in line throwing the life-giving liquid over the back of the Jellybot. Groans of ecstasy were coming out of his mouth as he enjoyed being spoilt for the whole day.

Others were marking out a clear pathway through the remaining spikes of the minefield to ensure the safety of all on the beach.

Tom and Clarissa, with the help of the Humming-bats, erected an ingenious system of ropes and pulleys up the side of the cliff to the entrance of the cave. There was a continuous stream of excited Cosywags who wanted to see for themselves the incredible picture of the Rainchild that Tom had discovered on the cave's wall.

Several volunteers, with Tom in charge, worked the pulley.

'One, two, three, heave! One, two, three, heave! One, two, three, heave!' It was extremely hard work, but all the effort was well worth it.

They would go up in groups of four in a basket. As one went up another was coming down. The difference in the mood of those in the up basket to those in the down basket was amazing.

Going up, there were excited squeals of laughter and a sense of expectation. The only quiet ones on the up journey were those who were scared of heights.

Coming down was a completely different story.

Each one, without exception, had been totally overwhelmed by the magnificent picture. Only somebody who had seen and met the Rainchild could have drawn such a picture. It went beyond artistic skill and had within it another dimension, a greater depth, a deeper meaning than any had encountered before.

As they got out of the basket, some were softly weeping, others looked as though they had seen a miracle. There were even those whose faces seemed to glow with a warmth that had not been there before.

New hope had begun to grow again in the lives of all the creatures on the beach. Everyone felt sorry for the Jellybot, for he was the only one who could not get to see the picture for himself, and yet he had been the one all along who was so sure the Rainchild was the answer. His faith had never weakened even though his body had become almost useless.

'I wonder how the pictures got there,' said Tom, quickly steadying the final stages of a basket landing.

'It must have been our ancestors,' answered Clarissa. 'At one time the waters of the Crystal Sea were so deep that they reached up to the top of the cliff. The cave must have been a home for someone living under the sea.'

'Where did all the water go?' asked Tom curiously. 'After all, the Purple Plug was only stolen a few days ago. The water can't have gone down that much in such a short time.'

Clarissa was clear in her answer.

'Ever since our people turned their backs on the Rainchild and the sacred writings, rapid evaporation has taken place all over the sea. We have seen very little rain, so the waters never get a chance to be replenished. This has been going on for hundreds of years. The theft of the Purple Plug has made us all realise our desperate plight, but the problem has been going on without us even noticing it for a long time. That's the tragedy of it all! How could we have been so blind?'

'Don't upset yourself,' said Tom tenderly. 'Everything is going to be all right.'

The baskets continued trundling up and down until a sudden jerk of the rope brought both baskets unexpectedly to a halt. They were both crammed full of passengers and were swinging precariously halfway up to the cave which was at least twelve metres from the ground.

In one sense it was a very amusing sight. The baskets were swinging side by side at the cross-over point. The passengers in the one on the way down showed no sign of panic, but sat there gazing out to sea with a look of awe on their faces. They were still bathing in the wonder of their moments with the picture and were hardly aware of what was going on.

The passengers in the other basket were not so calm — rather the reverse! They were hanging over the edge of the basket, looking down at Tom and Clarissa saying things like, 'What's going on down there? Don't you know we're stuck?'; 'I never did trust these new fangled scientific contraptions!'; and 'Help! I feel sea sick!'

Tom couldn't help bursting out into fits of laughter at the last one. 'Keep your eye on the horizon and keep rowing!' he called back in a playful voice.

'This is no time for joking,' reprimanded Clarissa, who was also looking decidedly worried.

Tom sent the Hummingbats up to the top of the rope where the two pulleys were connected to the rock. The fluorescent blue colouring in their wings was dazzling as all eyes looked up at them to see if they could solve the problem. Something had probably got jammed in one of the wheels and it just needed cleaning out, they reported. No problem.

Meanwhile the situation in the 'up' basket was getting worse.

One of the Cosywags stuck his leg over the side and was trying to reach the other basket. Either he had had enough and wanted to get his feet back on the ground as soon as possible, or he couldn't stand the near hysterics of the others in his basket! The trouble was, as he did so, the whole thing started leaning over to one side. There was nearly a riot. The basket started swinging more violently. Now Tom was getting worried.

'Stay calm!' he pleaded. 'We'll have you down in no time!'

The panic continued. Then one of the Cosywags called down to Tom. 'I'm going to jump!' she yelled.

Now it was Tom's turn to panic. 'Stay where you are!' he shouted.

'No, I'm coming right now!' she said in a determined voice, and then added, 'And you had better catch me, young Tom!'

By now a rather bemused crowd had gathered and were looking up at the dangerously swinging basket with the little Cosywags scrambling over the edge and getting ready to jump.

Tom was running backwards and forwards with his arms outstretched, trying to stay underneath the thing. He was terrified that he might trip over something and miss the jumping creature.

Realising he had no choice but to go along with it, Tom shouted, 'Jump after the count of three!'

The crowd held its breath.

Tom felt like a fielder in a cricket match — but he never was any good at cricket!

'One, two …'

Before he could get to three, the little Cosywag lost her balance and came tumbling down through the air.

Sighs of relief rippled through the audience as Tom caught the Cosywag in his arms, swinging them in a downward motion to break the impact of the fall. There was a spontaneous outburst of applause and cheering which made Tom feel a little embarrassed.

Suddenly the ropes jerked again and both baskets started moving. The Hummingbats had done their repair job quickly and efficiently.

At the end of the day Tom and Clarissa went back to a shelter for something to eat. As they walked across the beach, Tom was thinking that he must have used up as much nervous energy during the drama with the jumping Cosywag, as he had the day before during the battle with the Sandmen!

'That Cosywag had a lot of faith in me, you know,' he reflected. 'If only we could have that kind of faith in the Rainchild.'

There was a sudden whooshing sound and Tom ducked, pushing Clarissa to the ground at the same time.

'Ouch!' she said. 'What is the matter with you!?'

'We're under attack!' he yelled. 'Take cover!'

Clarissa stood up and looked down at Tom. He was rolled up in a tight ball with both arms wrapped round his head and his bottom stuck up in the air.

She burst into fits of laughter.

'Take cover, you stupid Cosywag!' mumbled Tom.

'You think I'm stupid, do you? Have you looked at yourself lately?'

Tom uncovered one eye and looked up.

'There's nothing to worry about,' said Clarissa, 'it's only the Slickwingers arriving. They are our friends from the other side of the ocean. They are going to help us to fly!' she said triumphantly.

'What!' said Tom, jumping to his feet.

He ducked again quickly as three Slickwingers zoomed close over their heads. There was a crash and a thud as one of them went straight through a beach shelter. Fortunately, these were made out of dried foliage supported by lengths of stalk and cane, so it collapsed easily on impact. This was good news for big birds doing a crash landing, but not such good news for those who might be inside!

They ran over, together with half the Cosywags on the beach, to see what had happened.

No one was hurt, but the shelter had collapsed on one side where the creature had sliced straight through a supporting cane, and there, a few metres further on, was a funny sight.

The Slickwinger had pinned himself to a soft part of the cliff face by his long pointed beak and was trying desperately to push himself away using his webbed feet up against the cliff face.

'And *they* are going to help *us* to fly?' said Tom. 'They need to get their own act together first!'

'Aww! Oooh! Haaa! Errg!'

'I think he's trying to say something,' said Tom sarcastically.

'Come on, give me a hand,' said Clarissa.

They got both sides of the gigantic bird-like creature and began to pull for all they were worth. He was much bigger than Tom first thought: at least two metres long, not counting the beak. There was no telling how long that was as most of it was still stuck in the cliff face!

He had beautiful blue feathers all over his body, with dark blue stripey patterns on his wings. Again it was difficult to estimate, but Tom reckoned his full wing span must have been at least four metres. Quite impressive. But not so impressive in this embarrassing position!

They tugged and pulled, and suddenly all three fell over backwards as the huge bird broke loose from the cliff. There were wings and feathers everywhere for a few moments while they scrambled to their feet and looked at one another in silence. At exactly the same moment, they all started laughing uncontrollably. The sound the Slickwinger was making as he laughed made everyone laugh even more. It was a high-pitched gurgling sound, and his neck was wobbling up and down frantically.

'Sorry about that,' said the Slickwinger apologetically. 'My name's Baz, but you can call me Slick for short.'

Tom wondered what 'Slick' had to do with 'Baz', but he didn't bother to ask.

'I'm here to give you a hand,' said Baz, 'or rather a wing!' He started gurgling again and his laughter was infectious.

Finally getting herself under control, Clarissa said, 'Well, Baz, I think we ought to ...' She was interrupted by Baz.

'Oh do call me "Slick",' he said. 'It suits my personality much better than "Baz". You know what I mean ... fast, efficient, impressive ...'

'... clumsy, careless, crazy,' continued Tom.

'And who might you be?' enquired Slick, looking Tom straight in the eye.

The next couple of hours were spent eating and drinking and telling Slick all that had happened in the last few days. They sat on the warm sand near the Jellybot as they were concerned that he also should be included in this new development. Slick didn't look in the least surprised when they told him about the new-found swimming skills of the Cosywags, and how they could survive under water. His elegant, confident looks bore no comparison to his unruly crash landing earlier that day, and he seemed to know already all the things he was being told.

Then, with a regal look on his face, he stunned them all with one simple statement.

'I'm here because the Rainchild sent for me.'

He paused to allow the truth to sink in, then continued.

'All last night, Princess Amathena was in contact with the Rainchild. Her words, which she spoke out into the night, were carried by the sea wind up to the golden cloud. The Rainchild always acts upon words spoken in simplicity and sincerity, and as a result of her expressing the desires which are in all your hearts, I have been sent to help. Oh, yes,' he continued, almost as an afterthought, 'I've got some of my friends with me as well.'

Yes, they were all aware of that.

They had flown in like the Red Arrows out of the sun, in perfect formation, until things went a bit wrong with the landing! There were at least eight of them, now being given welcome hospitality by the rest of the Cosywags.

For one naughty moment, Tom couldn't help thinking that the Rainchild must have a tremendous sense of humour, sending Slick along to help!

The Jellybot, who had been quietly taking all this in, spoke up. 'I know what you're thinking, Tom, but never forget that it is surprising how the most unlikely people get involved in the most daring exploits!'

Tom looked at him with a knowing grin on his face, realising that the Jellybot was referring to him. There was much more to that lovable lump of jelly than met the eye, he thought.

'You're right!' said the Jellybot. Tom nearly fell of his seat with surprise!

The crowds of Cosywags, who up until this

moment had been sitting in clumps chatting excitedly, began to form into two long rows, creating an aisle right across the beach. Down through the middle came Princess Amathena, walking sedately and serenely towards Slick and the others. Tom's heart seemed to take a leap and he suddenly felt like a lump of jelly. He knew how the Jellybot must feel now! He was staggered by her beauty. She was human in form, but there was something very different about her that made it obvious she was from another world.

Tom had never been in love with a girl before, so he wasn't quite sure how it was supposed to feel. He was certain that this could be it. Either that, or he was catching the flu!

'Hello, Slick,' she said warmly, 'how are you?'

'Very well, thank you,' he said respectfully.

They obviously knew each other.

'The Slickwingers have a very special relationship,' she said, addressing everybody, with a quietly commanding voice. 'They have access to the Golden Cloud and the presence of the Rainchild himself. As his messengers they have been alive for a thousand years. We are privileged to receive their help in our battle against the evil Megagrit.'

She paused, as if waiting for a reaction. Everyone stayed quiet, hanging on to every word she spoke.

'We want an army of volunteers,' she continued, 'to go with us on the dangerous mission to get back the Purple Plug. It will take too long to travel over land and in any case it is unlikely that we could survive the journey across the salt flats and the burning desert, so the Slickwingers are going to help us to fly.'

Tom had heard this already from Clarissa and he

still couldn't believe it. The little Cosywags had enough trouble going up a few metres in a basket. How ever would they cope with flying through the sky?

Amathena noticed the disbelieving look on Tom's face, but made no comment. She continued with her speech.

'We are going to construct large baskets which the Slickwingers will carry using ropes slung over their backs.'

Oh no, thought Tom, not more baskets!

'There will be some test flights to find out how many each basket will hold and how well Slick and his friends can handle the situation.'

Tom suddenly had a vivid picture in his mind of Slick, pinned to the side of the cliff by his beak, and panicking Cosywags hanging on to a crashed basket for all they were worth.

'When we are satisfied with the arrangements,' continued Princess Amathena, 'our journey to Megagrit and the battle for the Plug will begin. How many of you are with me?' she asked.

Every paw on the beach went up with excited enthusiasm.

They don't know what they are letting themselves in for, thought Tom, slowly raising his hand.

7

Flight Into the Desert

It had become apparent that Brutus and his Clawhammer comrades had not been seen for at least twenty-four hours.

A lot had happened in that time. There had been the terrifying battle with the three Sandmen, leaving the poor Cosywags frightened and demoralised; there was Tom's discovery of the cave and the picture of the Rainchild; Princess Amathena had arrived and caused a real stir, especially for Tom, and then there was the moving ceremony of the burning of the Gusters. But now, the incredible entrance that Slick had made on the scene and the Princess's revelations about him had changed what seemed to be an impossible dream into an opportunity to bring the glory back to the land of Crystalan.

No one was aware of the tragic drama that had been going on at the castle of Megagrit, leaving several Clawhammers dead, and Bruno feeling a failure.

It was the problem of not knowing that clinched it for Brutus.

He could not bear to sit around any longer waiting for news of his brother. In his usual impulsive fashion he had left, well before dawn, with two others still able to make the gruelling journey in search of their comrades. They were now already halfway across the salt flats. Brutus hoped that they could get to the castle without too much exposure to the devastating heat of the sun in the desert. The small party of determined Clawhammers were doing it the hard way, on foot. You had to admire their courage, even if they were a little unruly at times. Of course, they had no idea that soon, they would be overtaken by a bunch of flying Cosywags!

Back on the beach, preparations were being made for the first test flight. Tom was sitting on a rock by the edge of the sea, mesmerised by the sparkling waters before him. He had always loved the sea. It was so big and awesome, and it inspired him to think about great things and escape some of the more trifling issues of his young life.

However, today, as he stared at the water, he could not get his mind free from doubt.

'This is never going to work,' he muttered to himself. 'Those big birds might be great in the air, but everyone knows that it is the take-off and landing that are the crucial moments of any flight.'

He picked up a stone on the beach and threw it into the sea. It skipped along the top of the water and disappeared into the deep. Suddenly looking more interested, he picked up another stone with a flat bottom and threw it low out over the waters. It skimmed along much further than the first stone and gently slowing down, came to a stop before sinking to the bottom.

'That could be the way!'

He quickly grabbed another flat stone nearby, determined to test the idea that was coming into his mind. With a low sweeping motion of his arm, he threw the stone into the inviting waters. Just as before, it glided along the top of the gentle waves as if deciding for itself where to land, and then touched down slowly sinking into the depths below.

'That is definitely the answer! I must tell Slick!'

He was still talking excitedly to himself as he ran up the beach to where Slick and Clarissa were directing operations. It's quite difficult to run on soft sand because the ground seems to give way underneath you with every step. He took a couple of tumbles on the way, but hardly noticed them, as with every moment the idea seemed to him to be a dead cert!

He soon arrived at the scene where Slick was in the middle of giving some vital instructions to the Cosywag volunteers on the best way to construct the baskets for the flight.

'I've got a great idea about how to land those baskets in the desert!' he shouted, cutting right into the little lecture that was going on. Everyone automatically turned towards Tom and went, 'Sssshh!'

'Please be quiet for a moment,' countered Slick, 'I'm just about to tell them how to make the bottom of the baskets. They've got to be safe for the take-off and landing. These are the most vital moments of the flight!'

Slick turned to the Cosywag workers. 'Make sure the bottoms are flat, wide and slightly turned up around the edges. The take-off and landing will be much smoother that way.'

He turned towards Tom and gave a knowing wink!

'You do know what you are doing after all,' said Tom. 'I do apologise.'

'Oh, that's all right,' said Slick. 'I'm sure I'll make a few mistakes before this day's out!'

Tom joined in with the test flight preparations and they soon had the first large square basket ready. Made in a similar way to the shelters on the beach, with dried leaves interwoven with strong roots and cane, it could hold ten Cosywags plus a large container of water. Four lengths of rope made out of twine tightly knitted together, were attached to the corners and they were joined at the top by a large metal ring.

These rings had been ingeniously obtained by cutting links off the chain of the Plug, the remains of which were still lying on the bottom of the ocean. It was quite a tricky operation, swimming down to the sea bed, carefully avoiding the pull of the whirlpool. Some of the Cosywags who had been down before had volunteered for the job, even though they knew how dangerous it would be and how upsetting. Wreckage from one of the Gusters which had been caught by the whirlpool would bring back heartbreaking memories. They had bravely undertaken the mission and although many were deeply distressed, they had brought back the rings which were the vital keys to success.

The eight Slickwingers were to wear a specially designed harness over their backs, from which would dangle a hook, also cleverly adapted from chain links. The passengers in the basket would hold up the ring as high as they could, and the Slickwinger would do a low fly past, connecting the hook with the ring. For the landing, there was a smaller piece of rope attached to the hook, which the Slickwinger would hold in his beak. At the chosen moment, he would pull on the rope, raising the hook and causing the ring to slip off. The birds would have to judge their speed and height very accurately, so that the basket would skim along the ground and come to a safe halt.

A well thought-out design, but it would take some practice before they could be confident in going ahead with their mission. Lives depended on it.

'I'll try it first,' said Slick, having the harness fixed to his body. 'I'll need a run up of at least ten metres before I can get in the air. Are all preparations for the runway completed?'

One of the Cosywags had been appointed 'foreman' for the vital task of smoothing off a long stretch of the firmer sand nearer the sea. He shuffled up to Slick.

'All OK, sir. We've thoroughly checked every inch of that runway and removed any bits of stone or rock that might impede your progress. Make sure you don't go outside the markers and you'll be fine, sir.'

Slick looked down the length of the makeshift runway and took note of the carefully laid line of stones down each side, marking precisely the line of take-off.

He turned to Tom.

'There will be no passengers this time round, so would you hold the ring up for me? And please keep your hand steady on the fly past.'

Tom was doubtful, to say the least, but so much work had been put in that he felt he had to make some sort of effort. He and several of the Cosywags dragged the empty basket three quarters of the way down the runway, and the first test run was about to begin. Crowds of Cosywags lined the runway on each side, carefully staying beyond the stone markers. The Hummingbats had the best view, perched on top of some reasonably high rocks at the end of the runway. Some of the onlookers buried their heads in their hands; they couldn't bear to look. The tension mounted, and the atmosphere was excited.

Tom grabbed the ring and, standing to one side of the basket, held it up as high as he could. Slick, complete with harness, walked slowly away from the basket, measuring out a rough distance of about fifteen metres. He turned and took a deep breath. Every eye was on the big bird.

'Give me a countdown, Tom. On zero, I'll start my run.'

'Ten, nine, eight, seven ...'

Gradually everyone joined in the count till there was a great crescendo of voices.

'... six, five, four, THREE, TWO, ONE, ZERO!'

There was a spray of sand as Slick moved off from a standing position and started his run. His big webbed feet carried him along with a 'thump, thump, thump,' and the ground vibrated. With an expression of intense concentration and determination on his face, Slick gathered speed down the runway. He got within three metres of the basket and broke the stunned silence with a screech of panic. 'Abort! Abort! Out of the way! I can't get off the ground!'

There was a creaking and snapping as Slick collided ungracefully with the basket and came to a standstill half in and half out of it.

Tom tried not to laugh, but he couldn't help it. Everybody joined in, tentatively at first, for they were not sure whether they ought to laugh under the circumstances. But it certainly broke the tension of the moment.

'If at first you don't succeed, try, try and try again!' said Tom.

For the second time in three days he wished he hadn't used a well-known saying at the wrong moment.

'You're right, Tom,' said Slick, desperately untangling himself from this undignified situation. 'The problem is, the hook dangling underneath me is making it hard to build up enough speed. It's dragging along the sand. If I allow a few extra metres I should be able to manage it.'

'You'll manage it,' said the Jellybot confidently, 'the Rainchild is with you!'

There was a respectful silence for a few minutes as they all remembered why they were here and how vital their mission was.

Slick stepped slowly back to his starting point, then moved back another three metres.

'Ready, everyone?' he shouted. 'Forget the countdown. I'll just do it this time.'

He was off, getting faster with every step, those enormous wings stretched out to the full, and the air turbulence causing sand to fly up everywhere. It seemed painfully slow, but gradually his webbed feet left the ground, although they were still kicking, as if running on air. His wings took the strain and he began to rise.

'Hold the ring still!' he shouted to Tom, who by now had closed his eyes tightly. He came zooming past the basket, and the hook just failed to connect with the ring.

'I'll come straight round for a second try,' he

shouted, now high over the beach. He looked like a jumbo jet circling Heathrow Airport, as he flew at what seemed a dangerously slow speed then came in low for his next attempt.

It must have been very difficult to judge the position of the hook hanging beneath his body, so when there was the clank of metal against metal, and the basket began sliding along the ground and then slowly rising in the air, there was a tumultuous round of applause.

'Don't fly too low over that cliff edge,' shouted Tom. 'Remember you've got to allow much more clearance now.'

Slick resisted the temptation to tell him that he knew exactly what he was doing, and made a couple of circles round the beach before attempting a landing.

Flying in low, he pulled on the release rope and the ring slipped off the hook. The basket bounced along the sand for a few metres and came to a standstill.

The theory of the skimming stone definitely worked with the specially designed baskets.

The whole of that day, the Slickwingers worked hard, practising their takeoffs and landings with the baskets underneath them. There were a few near misses and minor injuries, but in the main, the day was a great success. That evening there was a carnival atmosphere, as all over the beach food and hot drinks were prepared at small fires for the tired workers, and already celebrations were going on in anticipation of a successful mission. The delightful smells of cooking food made Tom feel quite hungry, and he moved from one bonfire to the next, sampling the variety of interesting flavours on offer.

The real business would start the next day.

As the sun rose across the sea, Tom, the Cosywags, the Hummingbats and the Slickwingers were all hard at work, getting ready for the flight into the desert.

The water containers were filled and carefully loaded into the baskets by the Cosywag volunteers. After all the pre-flight checks had been done, including the testing of ropes, rings, hooks and harnesses, Tom, Princess Amathena and Clarissa climbed into the leading basket which would be carried by Slick himself. All the remaining Cosywags would stay back at the beach with the Jellybot, who seemed to be well in control of the situation even though he was not directly involved.

When everything was ready, Slick called everyone together. The princess stood next to him giving approving nods as he spoke.

'I am not going to deceive you, I want to be totally honest. The mission upon which we are about to embark is a most hazardous and ambitious operation. Attempting such a feat will take the utmost courage, commitment and concentration. Some of you may even sacrifice your lives, but our cause is honourable and just and we must not shrink from this vital task. It may be the last chance we have to ensure that our children grow up in a world dominated by good rather than evil, by freedom rather than bondage, by life rather than death, by love rather than hatred, by joy rather than sadness. We go to honour the name of the Rainchild and to restore the fortunes of Crystalan.'

There was a spontaneous clapping of paws as the Cosywags signalled their approval and dedication to the mission. Nobody underestimated the seriousness of the moment and they stood in silence for two minutes, each one coming to terms in his own heart with the prospect before them and the price to be paid.

Slick then shared with everybody the plan of action.

He spoke about the specific strategy which had been worked out with advice from the Jellybot, who had inside information on the workings of Megagrit and his evil kingdom. The Hummingbats were given the job of carrying the Purple Plug back to the Crystal Sea using the golden rope as soon as Megagrit had been dealt with.

The moment had come. The Cosywag volunteers got into their respective baskets which had been placed in position. All eight Slickwingers stood in line at the beginning of the runway. The big eyes of the Jellybot were wide open, giving approving looks of encouragement to the daring new airforce.

The order was given, and they were off.

A cloud of dust rose into the air as the big birds gathered speed and flew low towards their ringed targets. Each Slickwinger seemed to falter slightly as he took up the extra weight of the precious cargo in the baskets, but with slow determination and the strength of their impressive wings, they rose gracefully into the air.

Following the instructions of their pre-flight briefing, they flew out over the sea and then took a course parallel with the beach in order to gain the height necessary to clear the high cliff.

Slick glanced back to check that the take off was successful and noticed that there was still one basket on the ground. The worried occupants were holding the ring in the air, but the bird had missed and was coming round for a second attempt. Princess Amathena, Tom and Clarissa looked down and with bated breath, willed the bird to make the connection.

'You're coming in too fast!' shouted Slick.

A sudden cloud of dust blocked their view for a second, and they thought catastrophe had struck. Then, emerging through the dust, came the bird with the basket swinging precariously underneath, but he was heading straight for the cliff face.

'Turn out over the sea!' shouted Slick. 'You'll never get over the cliff first time with the extra weight you're carrying!'

From their vantage point above the scene, it looked as though the bird's angle of ascent would take him on a certain collision course with the cliff. The Slickwinger's huge wings cast an oversize shadow on the beach which suddenly shrank as the bird miraculously cleared the cliff top. The basket underneath scraped over the edge and sent loose rocks crashing to the ground below.

There was a sigh of relief as all eight birds, safely airborne, got into formation and turned out towards the salt flats.

The Hummingbats took up position at the rear and carried the golden rope between them using their strong sharp teeth. Some of the Cosywags had their eyes tightly closed while others were looking excitedly over the edge of their basket admiring the view. The Crystal Sea looked transparent and inviting, glittering like clusters of diamonds around a jewelled crown.

As they flew high over the beach, they took one last look at the Jellybot who was gazing up towards them with the same look of encouragement on his face. Everyone knew that even though he was not making the journey, he would still be with them. He was such an unwieldy and lonely figure, yet he seemed to give them added strength by his own courage and determination to win.

Slick had the most difficult job of all, for as the appointed leader of the expedition, not only did he carry the weight of responsibility on his shoulders but also the lives of his passengers. If anything happened to them, he would never forgive himself.

Trying to relieve the pressure a bit, he shouted back down the line of birds, 'No aerial acrobatics today, lads! Let's keep it straight and true!'

A gurgling sound rippled down through the feathered formation and soon they were flying over the hot desert sand.

There was silence for a long time. The only sound that could be heard was the powerful swish of the giant wings above them and the rush of the wind in their faces. Tom broke the silence.

'Look!' he shouted. 'It's Brutus and his friends!'

The three muscular creatures looked like ants, but their hammer-shaped heads were unmistakable, even from such a height.

'Seems they are going to the same place we are going,' retorted Clarissa, with a definite tone of disapproval in her voice.

'Yes, they are probably going to make another deal with their friend, Megagrit,' added Tom.

Amathena rarely used many words, but when she spoke, there always seemed to be a note of authority in her voice.

'Don't judge them too soon,' she said. 'The situation may be very different from the way it appears.'

Tom and Clarissa felt a little rebuked but deep down inside they knew the princess was right.

'Remember the plan,' shouted Slick. 'When we get near to our objective, make sure you approach with the sun behind you. That will give us maximum opportunity to take advantage of the element of surprise.'

As soon as he had spoken, the Castle of Megagrit appeared on the horizon. It looked menacing and impregnable and a wave of fear struck at the heart of each Cosywag.

'Don't be overwhelmed or intimidated by the sight of the castle,' shouted Slick, obviously realising how everybody was feeling. 'We have the power to defeat that evil monster.' Then, addressing himself to the other Slickwingers, he gave his command. 'Adjust your course, we fly out of the sun.'

The Sandmen would normally be very difficult to see from above, for their bodies were naturally camouflaged against the background of the sand, but so many of them had copied their master by sticking bits of mud and grit over their bodies, that they became easy targets for the Cosywag airforce.

At a prearranged signal from Slick, four of the big birds broke formation, and, diving at what seemed to be an impossible angle, swooped down over the vast open courtyard of the castle. The Cosywags in the baskets had the containers at the ready, and judging their distance and velocity perfectly tipped a continuous stream of water through a hole in the bottom of the basket.

Sandmen ran in all directions trying to avoid the downpour but as soon as the water touched them, they disintegrated and all that was left were bits of mud and grit. When the water touched anything that was in league with evil, destruction was inevitable.

Then Slick led the rest of the group down towards the courtyard. There was just enough room to make a landing outside the large stone doors leading into the audience room and Megagrit himself.

Taking hold of the release rope in their beaks, the remaining four birds came in low, just clearing the outside sand walls of the courtyard, and when the baskets were about half a metre from the ground, they gave a hard tug on the rope. The baskets hit the ground and skimmed along the surface of the sand for about five metres before coming to a halt. One of the baskets crash landed and tipped completely upside down, trapping its startled cargo underneath.

While ten Cosywags from another basket were attempting to lift one corner to release their friends, Amathena and Tom carried a heavy water container over to the stone door.

'Are you ready, Tom?' puffed Amathena, running out of breath.

Tom nodded.

They tipped the water out onto the base of the sand wall beside the door. It immediately began crumbling and falling away, and within seconds there was a clean cut hole into the audience room. A group of Cosywags were standing by with another container ready for any Sandman guards who might show up.

Strangely, everything seemed to have gone quiet.

Slick and the others were circling overhead, waiting for the signal to pick up their friends. The Hummingbats were ready with the golden rope to carry the Purple Plug back to the Crystal Sea. So far, things seemed to be going well.

Amathena, Tom, Clarissa and fifteen of the

Cosywags filed through the hole and into the audience room.

It took a few seconds for their eyes to adjust to the dimly lit room, but the situation very quickly became clear.

There was Megagrit, on the platform at the far end of the room, with the Purple Plug held high over his head. He had a contemptuous grin on his face as if he knew he had finally won.

'Take one more step towards me, and I will smash this precious Plug of yours before your very eyes!'

Tom let out a shriek of anger.

'You are a wicked monster! Why are you doing this? What do you hope to achieve?'

'Give me the princess. She will become my wife and share my kingdom.'

The flames from the torches on the corners of the platform seemed to add to the evil atmosphere of that moment.

'Well? What is your answer? She will be mine, the Plug will be yours. Think of all the little Cosywags you will save! Is this not a fair exchange?' His voice echoed round the large room.

Tom hesitated, not knowing what to do next.

Amathena whispered in his ear. 'We have no choice for the time being, but all is not lost. Here is what you must do.' She finished her secret message and before he could object, started walking towards Megagrit. Suddenly guards appeared from nowhere and ushered the princess up to the platform.

'Take her to my quarters,' yelled Megagrit, sensing victory.

Amathena looked back and gave a little wave to Tom and then was gone.

Megagrit, still standing with the Plug high in the air, let out a shriek of laughter that chilled the air and with a mighty whiplash of his strong arms, threw the Purple Plug to the ground, smashing it in pieces.

8

The Dark Chamber

Tom stood mesmerised by the sight for a few minutes. It was as if his feet were glued to the floor. He could not believe what his eyes were telling him. The Purple Plug, which was the key to the survival of the Jellybot and all his friends, was broken beyond repair.

It lay in pieces before him in the audience room of the Castle of Megagrit. Although the odds were highly unfavourable against Tom and the Cosywags, he was so incensed at the deceit of Megagrit, that he charged forward to the platform determined to get even.

The contents of the cauldron were still bubbling away and giving off a foul stench that was an offence to the nostrils. Tom leapt onto the empty platform with new agility, triggered by a sudden flow of adrenalin pumping through him. But Megagrit had disappeared down a ramp leading to a large stone door. Leaping down to the imposing barrier, he shouted as loud as he could.

'Megagrit! You coward! You deceiver! You will

never get away with it! I'll make sure you get what's coming to you! How could you be so cruel? Amathena is my friend, let her go right now, or else!'

The fire from the torches flickered, unconcerned at the dramatic events happening around them and the only sound that could be heard was the bubbling of the cauldron.

Tom became aware of Cosywags all around him looking sad and dejected. 'We've failed,' they said. 'We're all going to die.'

They spent the next half an hour examining the stone door through which Megagrit had disappeared and all around the area at the bottom of the platform.

It appeared that Megagrit's quarters were surrounded on all sides and on the top with solid stone. There was no way in.

With head in hands, Tom sat down with the Cosywags on the edge of the platform. There was a frightening atmosphere in the castle which made them feel cold and they began to shiver uncontrollably. Sensing the desperation and despondency in the forlorn looks of his Cosywag friends, Tom decided that enough was enough! They must all get moving and trust that the Rainchild would help them, even though the situation seemed hopeless.

After a while he spoke up with a new resolve in his voice.

'There is only one thing for it. I will have to do what the princess told me to do before she gave herself up.' And then turning to the Cosywags, who looked as if they had no fight left in them, he said, 'Come on! We've got no time to lose! And if that Megagrit harms one hair on the head of the princess, I will personally ...'

'Now, now, now,' said Clarissa, butting in, 'that's no way to talk. Violence is not the answer. Nobody ever won a war with violence.'

Tom couldn't figure out what she meant at the time, but he was later to understand.

They rushed out into the courtyard. There were no Sandmen to be seen. Slick and the other big birds were circling overhead with the Hummingbats, waiting for the signal.

'Where's the Plug?' shouted Slick.

'We've lost it for ever,' replied Tom, 'but we have another plan. Come and pick us up. We'll get into the baskets ready for takeoff.'

Slick seemed rather bewildered at this turn of events. This was not the way things were supposed to happen, but he thought he'd better go along with it. He was rather concerned that things get under way fairly quickly, as they would soon be hampered by failing light. He estimated that they had perhaps two hours of daylight left. So with Slick leading the way, the Slickwingers started coming round for their low approach and the pick-up of the baskets.

Everybody, apart from the princess, was now safely installed in the baskets, when suddenly a thumping sound came from the outside wall beyond the courtyard.

There was a thunderous crash as the wall crumbled and fell, and Brutus and his friends came scrambling through the gap. They had used their heads as battering rams, and they were obviously feeling sore and tired.

Brutus stomped straight up to Tom, who was sitting in the basket, and demanded, 'What is going on round here? We've just destroyed three

Sandmen. They told us that our comrades, including my brother Bruno are dead! Where is that double-crossing Megagrit? We had an agreement with him.'

He stared at Tom with a guilty look on his face and then, totally unexpectedly, broke down in floods of tears.

'We've made a terrible mistake,' he spluttered through the sobs. 'Why did we listen to that evil Megagrit in the first place? All we could think of was ourselves, and now we have betrayed the Jellybot and all the creatures of Crystalan! What are we going to do?'

Tom felt a lump in his throat. He never in a million years thought he would see a Clawhammer crying. It was obvious that beneath that cold, callous exterior, there was a heart of gold. Princess Amathena was right. Outward appearances could be very deceiving. Perhaps the Clawhammers had always been misunderstood because of their rather domineering shape and size.

Tom's immediate thoughts and feelings about Brutus and the others were about to be put to the test.

The big birds, with Slick in the lead, were making their final approach, having cleared the outer walls of the castle.

'Don't hold the rings up,' shouted Tom to everyone in the baskets, 'we're not going yet!'

The birds, seeing that there were no rings to link up to, zoomed overhead with surprised looks on their faces and came to land a short distance away near the opposite wall.

'Quick! Everyone gather together for a conference! We need some action round here,' shouted Tom with real urgency in his voice.

When everyone had gathered round, Tom, looking every inch the leader, explained that Bruno and the other Clawhammers had gone missing.

'We'll start a thorough search of the castle,' he said. 'Work in groups of ten and decide who is going to be the leader of your group. When you've done that, it is the leader's responsibility to make sure his group has a supply of water. If you are confronted by Sandmen, you know what to do!'

For the next few minutes there was a lot of chattering and moving to and fro, but eventually they all managed to sort themselves out into equally numbered groups.

Brutus and the other two Clawhammers joined Tom and Clarissa. The Slickwingers and the Hummingbats stayed on lookout duty overhead to warn of coming danger. The teams split up and the search began.

Tom and his group went back into the audience room and turned immediately right into a long, tubelike corridor. They found it difficult to walk on the floor because of its curved shape — little did they know that this very place had been the scene of a terrible battle only two days before.

Some way up the corridor, on the left-hand side, they found the remains of a large dormitory. The walls were smashed down and the sun was shining through a gaping hole in the roof where the ceiling had collapsed. They were just about to step through what once was a door into the room, when Brutus stopped in his tracks. He was looking with a fixed stare at the debris spilling out around his feet.

'What is it?' whispered Clarissa anxiously.

No words were necessary, for as they gathered

around, they could clearly see what they desperately hoped they would never find.

In the floor of the corridor there was an unmistakeable imprint of the shape of a Clawhammer's head. Each one in the little group stood silently mesmerised by the sight, as if to brace themselves for the inevitable discovery of the bodies of their Clawhammer friends.

Tom broke the silence. 'Listen!'

There was a strange rumbling noise, like the sound you hear when you are waiting for a tube train to come into the station.

'There's something coming down the corridor at great speed!'

'Quick! Into the dormitory!' said Clarissa in an urgent whisper.

They clambered over the remains of the wall and lay still in the dirt and sand. Three Sandmen came whizzing past them a matter of centimetres away, their bodies fitting snugly into the curved floor of the corridor.

Tom gave the all clear. 'There's nothing here. We have to go deeper into the castle. We must not give up the search until we are sure there is no hope of finding Bruno and the others.'

'I must go alone!' protested Brutus. 'He's my brother and they are my comrades. I cannot expect you to risk your lives for us, not after all we have done to harm you!'

'We've all made our mistakes,' said Clarissa calmly and thoughtfully. 'We never showed any friendship towards you and have never allowed you to feel cared for. Now we must care for one another. We're in this thing together. We won't leave you.'

For one moment Tom felt a little resentful. What

right did Clarissa have to speak on his behalf? After all, none of this crazy situation had anything to do with him in the first place! Why should he allow himself to get drawn into the inevitable end of all this? They would all lose their lives, and for what? The survival of strange creatures in a strange world full of strange goings-on!

'What's the matter, Tom?' whispered Clarissa discreetly.

'Oh, nothing,' said Tom. 'I was just thinking what a privilege it is to be part of this amazing adventure to save Crystalan!'

'Are you afraid?' she continued.

'Nothing further from my mind!' said Tom, trying to sound confident. He wondered how he could tell such bare-faced lies so easily.

Clarissa, sensing the situation, also wondered how he could tell such bare-faced lies so easily, but she let the matter drop. She realised how difficult it was for Tom. After all, he had already done so much for them. How could they expect more?

'I'm sorry,' said Tom. 'I *am* afraid, and I do wonder why I must be involved in such a crazy stunt as this. But deep down I know that there is a plan behind all this, and somehow I must be part of the answer.' Then, after a short pause, he continued reflectively, 'I am learning a lot about myself.'

'Let's get going,' said Clarissa.

They stepped back into the corridor and started along it. It was very dark as the sun could not penetrate into these inner areas of the castle. They hoped against hope that they would not be mown down by a speeding Sandman, for there was no immediate escape from the confines of that narrow space. Every step took them farther into the unknown and away from the comparative safety of the hole in the wall. It was very hot inside the corridors, and the air was stuffy and difficult to breathe. Tom's shirt was sticking to his body because of the perspiration all over him, and he felt really uncomfortable. He longed for a nice cold shower, or better still, a dip in the refreshing waters of the Crystal Sea. But all that seemed a million miles away from where they were now.

It had to happen sooner or later. The terrible rumbling sound could be heard in the distance, and a quick decision had to be made. Should they return as fast as possible back to the hole in the wall, or should they continue in the hope that there would be another opening? The Sandman was approaching fast.

Brutus made the decision with his feet. He pushed forward and forced his body into a clumsy jog. Thud! thud! thud! went his feet on the hard sand floor. The others followed as the sound grew louder and louder. Tom took up the rear and felt his heart pounding like a big bass drum with every faltering step.

Suddenly Brutus disappeared down an adjoining tunnel and shouted for the others to follow. Nobody needed telling twice. As Tom turned off the main corridor he felt a mighty gust of wind as the Sandman hurtled past and into the blackness. For a moment they all stood puffing and panting, but with a sense of relief. So far so good.

They continued down their new route and found that it was a dead end.

'There must be a way through,' whispered Clarissa.

'There is,' answered Brutus with a note of determination in his voice. 'I've found a door here, but it seems to have been sealed with large amounts of mud reinforced with grit and stone.'

'I wonder . . .' Tom's voice trailed off into silence as they all shared the same thought. Could it be that they had found what they were looking for? Had Bruno and the others been imprisoned in this ghastly tomb? If they were able to break down the door, what would they find? They dared not think about it.

Instinctively, they all gathered round in a tight circle to discuss a plan of action.

Meanwhile, Slick had been circling for over thirty minutes and there was no sign of anything moving down on the ground. Then suddenly he was aware of a commotion in the courtyard. The baskets were still in position, still free of occupants, but there were at least twenty Cosywags running around in what seemed to be utter confusion.

'What are they playing at?' muttered Slick to himself. And then the answer dawned on him. They had positioned themselves in careful formation in the shape of the letter 'B'.

'That's it!' he exclaimed. 'Right, lads. Remember our battle plans that we discussed before leaving base?'

There were nods of acknowledgement from the other Slickwingers and the Hummingbats.

'We are switching to Plan B. Search for the marker!'

Tom was so grateful for the piece of silver paper he had found in his trouser pocket. Packets of sweets had more than one use for those with a little imagination and enterprise.

In fear and trepidation at what they might find, they had broken through the reinforced door at the end of the tubeway using some more of the precious supplies of water they had with them. They had used more than they could really afford, but the surrounds of the door were tough and it took some time before the water could penetrate.

Eventually, however, the door came crashing down to reveal a dark empty space. A chute had been constructed, obviously for the use of Sandmen, as it had a curved bottom, and it fell away at what seemed an impossibly acute angle into the darkness. One by one, in an act of incredible bravery, they had slid down the chute and found themselves in a chamber.

A dazzling shaft of light came down through a small hole in the roof. They were in the castle dungeons. All around there were the remains of Sandmen who had obviously fallen into disfavour with the evil Megagrit and had paid the ultimate price. There was very little air and the stench was foul, but they had found what they were looking for.

Tom was never to forget that moment when Brutus saw his brother and the other Clawhammers huddled in a corner together. They looked a pathetic sight. The Cankor disease had grotesquely disfigured their faces, but miraculously they were alive. A tear ran down Tom's cheek as he watched the loving reunion of old friends and family. He was continually surprised and impressed by the Clawhammers' ability to show love and concern.

Realising that retracing their steps was impossible — especially if they were to get the injured and sick Clawhammers out to safety — Brutus and his two friends formed a tower, using their own bodies, reaching up to the ceiling. Tom was scared of heights, but he volunteered to climb to the top. He had gradually worked his way upwards, being careful to avoid causing any unnecessary discomfort to the supporting Clawhammers. Then, standing on the shoulders of Brutus, he stretched to his full height. It was highly dangerous and very precarious, but all thought of personal cost had disappeared completely from Tom's mind.

Somehow, Tom had managed to get his hand through the small air hole in the roof and was just about able, using the full length of his arm, to push right through to the outside, where he placed the small piece of silver paper.

That had been the most dangerous moment of all for the amateur acrobatic company. For when Tom's arm went into the hole, the chamber had become pitch black. The supporting Clawhammers, as strong as they were, almost lost balance, becoming disorientated in the sudden darkness.

Tom hoped that Clarissa had found her way safely back to the courtyard, and managed to get the vital message to Slick.

All they could do now was wait.

By now the sun was beginning to get fairly low in the sky, but there was still plenty of light to reflect on a piece of silver paper. As soon as he saw the bright reflection, Slick got his airborne troops into position. In perfect formation, side by side, they swooped down towards their target, beaks at the ready. With very little water at their disposal, this was their only hope of breaking through the roof to where Tom and the others were waiting.

Slick was used to getting his beak stuck into things, but this time, it was serious business. All eight birds struck at exactly the same moment, as if they had rehearsed the event on numerous occasions. Their beaks penetrated deeply into the sand making a line of perforations in the roof of the chamber. Using their strong webbed feet, they pushed themselves free and launched themselves into the air for a second hit.

Next time round they made an incredibly accurate line of perforations exactly parallel to the first line. Then they began to jump up and down between the two lines and sure enough, the roof gave way in a crash of sand, dust and grit. Peering down through the hole, they could see Tom, Brutus, the other Clawhammers, and Bruno with his injured companions. They had their hands over their eyes, dazzled by the sudden bright light as the roof opened up.

The Hummingbats were next on the scene. They lowered their golden rope through the gaping hole and hauled each one to the comparative safety of the courtyard where several Cosywags were still on guard, containers of water at the ready, in case of unwelcome intruders.

It was a slow and painful operation.

As Bruno and his friends appeared out of the chamber, with the golden rope securely wrapped around them, the full extent of their horrible ordeal could be seen. Only three of them had survived. Their bodies looked old and tired and were marked all over by the rapid advance of the crippling disease. They had come here to find a cure, but had instead discovered the terrible truth, that Megagrit had only evil on his mind and had no intention of helping them.

The three injured Clawhammers were helped into the waiting baskets, and as many Cosywags as could find room clambered in around them. Only seven of the eight baskets were operational, as the one which had crash landed was unsafe, so taking off would be difficult and hazardous with all the extra weight of the Clawhammers.

Tom managed to find Clarissa and they jumped into the leading basket and gave the order to hold the rings up high for the advancing Slickwingers.

Suddenly, from every direction, Sandmen were rolling towards them. At first they came tentatively, for fear of the water, but then, noticing that very little water was left, they gained courage and advanced with speed.

If Slick and the other birds did not connect with their rings first time, there would be little hope for those left behind. With the light fading rapidly and the threatened onslaught from the Sandmen, the chances of success were slim.

As the big birds swooped low over the courtyard ready for the pick up, Tom noticed to his horror that the hook which had been attached to Slick's harness was missing.

Slick, now within ten metres of the basket, shouted, 'Keep the ring still, I'm going to slide it over my beak!'

At the very last second, every basket rose into the air and cleared the castle wall.

Slick had managed to slide his beak into the ring, but was finding it almost impossible to keep his head straight because of the immense weight of the basket.

'Are you OK?' shouted Tom from underneath.

No answer came.

'Slick, are you all right?'

Tom suddenly realised that it would be impossible for Slick to speak, because he was unable to open his beak.

He felt the basket jerk with a forward motion. Then there was another jerk, and another. Slick was desperately fighting to stay in the air and keep his head upright, but the ring was slowly slipping off the end of his beak.

Suddenly Clarissa and the other Cosywags in the baskets screamed and Tom felt as though he had left his stomach behind as the basket went crashing down towards the ground a hundred metres below.

Many thoughts flashed through Tom's mind in a split second.

What would become of Princess Amathena in the evil hands of Megagrit? He had told no one her whispered message to him, so they would not know what to do to save Crystalan if he were to die!

Where was the Rainchild in all this? Why didn't he save them? Surely, after all they had gone through, this was not the way it should end?

9

The Riddle of the Sacred Anemone

Bracing themselves for the impact, the passengers in the falling basket huddled close together as they hurtled with gathering speed towards their doom.

The speed of the fall caused everything in the basket to shoot upwards and the wind whistled menacingly through every crack and gap in the fragile home-made craft. Everybody hung on tightly to the sides as this dramatic and unexpected turn of events threatened to become a tragedy of immense proportions.

The ring was blowing wildly in the air as if it was trying to find something to grip to. The tranquillity of a silent sunset seemed to emphasise the frantic activity of this moment of terror.

Then, suddenly, they slowed down and stopped in mid-air. It was the kind of feeling sky divers would experience if their parachute opened just in time for a safe landing. Not a word was uttered by anybody, as in a shocked silence they sat and waited to discover their fate.

It was a miraculous turn of events. One of the Slickwingers, left without a basket to carry back because of the one that had been damaged, was flying low as support should anything go wrong. It was a one in a million chance that he should be able to get his hook successfully connected to the loose ring of the falling basket, especially as visibility was getting worse by the minute — the sun looked as if it was performing a balancing act on the horizon and would soon give way to the night — but somehow the big bird managed it.

Only the Rainchild could have enabled the bird to do such an incredible thing under such impossible conditions.

The Slickwinger now carrying Tom, Clarissa, and a load of Cosywags took up first position in the line and Slick, relieved that his passengers were all safe, fell in behind.

'Change course and head for the Hanging Rock,' shouted Tom to his driver.

'Are you sure that is a wise decision, sir?' said the Slickwinger. 'It's at least half an hour further over the Crystal Sea beyond the beach and we would not get there until well into the night!'

Tom felt important for one moment. He had never been called 'sir' before.

'Yes, that's what we must do. The Princess has given me clear instructions. Send word back that the baskets carrying the injured and sick Claw-hammers should go back to the beach. Some of the Cosywags can go with them to help in any way they can.'

The message was passed back and three of the Slickwingers broke formation and headed off to the shelter of the beach. The remaining four, plus Slick, flew out over the sea and into the night towards the Hanging Rock.

No one had ventured near the Rock in living memory, although legends spoke of the weird and wonderful encounters many had experienced as a result of visiting the place. It was recognised as being the special home of the Sacred Anemone who lived in the water underneath its hanging arches.

Tom had been silent for a long time. He had watched the sun gradually sinking below the horizon, and the beautiful shades of light patterns caused by the changing shapes in the sky.

'I have been told to make contact with the Sacred Anemone,' he said, as if waiting for a reaction.

Slick drew up alongside the hanging basket. 'Before you can know the secrets you seek, you will be severely tested,' he said, with a serious expression on his face. 'Make sure your motives are right and your heart is clean before you attempt to approach the Sacred Anemone; nothing can be hidden from it.'

Tom wondered how you could clean your heart without taking it out, then realised that Slick was referring to his inner life, the part of him that went beyond mere bodily functions to something much deeper.

He had never thought very much about that sort of thing before. It was not the sort of thing you could think about unless you were faced with certain situations. Perhaps this was one of them. If Slick was right, he had some thinking to do.

It was getting quite dark now, and the silvery grey of the sky was smudged with patches of crimson where the sun had been. Without warning the Hanging Rock appeared in front of them as if it had risen out of the sea. It was completely surrounded by water, the nearest mainland being some twenty minutes flying time away, and the jagged rock had an unwelcoming look about it as if to ward off strangers. It came to a point at the top, and on one side stretched over the sea like a half-finished archway.

'There is nowhere for us to land,' shouted Slick. 'We'll drop your basket into the water and the Cosywags with you will be able to jump out and push you to a safe mooring in the shelter of the rock. We'll leave the Hummingbats with you to make sure you get back safely. Be careful!'

Tom wasn't too sure about getting wet after his first experience in the Crystal Sea, but it seemed the only option, and he had to make contact with the Sacred Anemone, so it had to be done.

They flew low over the water and the Slickwinger who had done such a gallant job in saving their lives released the basket. It skimmed across the surface of the water and came to rest a few metres from the side of the rock. The Cosywags immediately jumped out and began paddling as hard as they could, pushing the basket along in front of them until it came under the hanging part of the rock and a fairly safe harbour. They used some of the twine from the basket to tie it securely to some bits of rock jutting out from the side. By the time they climbed back in, they were quite exhausted.

'Now what?' they all said in unison.

The basket was gently bobbing up and down in the ebb and flow of the water, and Tom felt an irresistible urge to close his eyes and go to sleep. But there was work to be done, decisions to be made and a world to save. No time for sleep!

'Princess Amathena told me that if I made contact with the Sacred Anemone, he would be able to reveal the pathway ahead. She said he was a representative of the Rainchild and could pass on his wisdom and strength. He is the one who manufactured the silvery freedom dust, which is so valuable and liberating. She told me no more than that because we ran out of time. I must discover the rest for myself.'

The Cosywags listened with a look of wonder on their faces. They were rediscovering a lost heritage, and slowly the pieces were fitting together and making a lot of sense.

'You look after the basket and keep watch,' said Tom. 'I'm going to take a dive to see what I can find down there.'

Before another word could be spoken, Tom had taken a deep breath and disappeared under the water in a circle of white foam and bubbles.

He dived straight down, staying close to the side of the rock to keep his bearings. It was quite murky, although there was something refreshing and clean about the water that made Tom feel elated and alive. He began circling the rock to see if he could find what he was looking for. After one minute and ten seconds he had to get back to the surface to take in more air, then back down he went. He did this three or four times but still found nothing.

Although it was very dark on the surface by now, under the water there were tiny shafts of light darting in all directions like tiny laser beams. Tom guessed that these came from the particles of silvery freedom dust that seemed to be floating in abundance in the waters surrounding the rock.

He decided he'd go down one more time and then, if he still could not find the Sacred Anemone, he would have to get back to the basket and ask the Hummingbats to escort them back to the beach. Then they could resume the search the following day.

Diving under for the fifth time, he became suddenly aware that the tiny beams of light were getting more and more intense. He rounded a gigantic piece of rock that jutted out and then was confronted by a dazzling sight.

For a moment he closed his eyes to adjust to the light and immediately had the strange feeling of being suspended in mid-air. He had felt that way once before, so it was no surprise when he opened his eyes to discover that he was inside a huge air bubble. He could see outside very clearly, and there, sitting on a large platform-shaped stone that projected from the side of the rock, was the most beautiful sea anemone he had ever seen. Not that he had seen many in real life: most of them had been in pictures or in nature programmes on the television.

'Hello, I've been expecting you.'

Tom could hear the voice as clearly as if he had heard it through headphones. He remembered the Jellybot using that phrase when he first arrived at Crystalan. It seemed a lifetime ago now, but in fact it was only a matter of days.

He had obviously made contact with the Sacred Anemone.

Its tentacles, which must have numbered hundreds of thousands, were swaying with the movement of the water and shone with gold, deep red, and fluorescent blues and greens which were breathtaking in their beauty. Its body seemed almost transparent and reflected all the colours of the rainbow as the shafts of light from the silvery crystals danced around its form.

The voice spoke clearly and directly to him again.

'Er, excuse me, don't like to bother you too much, but are you with us?'

Tom seemed lost for words which was highly unusual for him. 'I ... I ... I am pleased to m-meet you, sir,' he stammered.

'Don't call me "sir"! I am a being, not a sir or a madam. I am a creature utterly different from anything you have come across before in your short life. It would take far too long to explain the whys and the wherefores, so we'll just get straight down to business.'

The Sacred Anemone paused for a moment as if preparing to utter the most amazing and significant statement ever spoken in the history of the universe.

'I want you to say the following phrase five times in quick succession. "I KNOW AN ANEMONE NAMED ANONA." Right, that's it! Off you go!'

Tom couldn't believe what he was hearing. He was expecting some deeply profound message and all he got was a tongue twister.

'Well, come on, I'm waiting!' said the Sacred Anemone, sounding a little agitated.

Tom took a deep breath. 'I know an anenena ... I know an anemenem ... I know an anemenenena ... I know an anenena naned anonona ... I naned an anononen knowed anenen ...'

'Come on, try harder!' encouraged the Anemone.

Slowly and deliberately Tom started the sentence again. 'I know an anemone named Anona.'

'Brilliant!' shouted the Anemone. 'Now say it faster!'

It was very frustrating for Tom in the circumstances, but with patience and determination he finally made it.

'I KNOW AN ANEMONE NAMED ANONA. I KNOW AN ANEMONE NAMED ANONA. I KNOW AN ANEMONE NAMED ANONA. I KNOW AN ANEMONE NAMED ANONA. I KNOW AN ANEMONE NAMED ANONA.'

There was a massive round of applause that sounded remarkably like ten thousand people at the Royal Albert Hall.

'Bravo, Tom!' said the Sacred Anemone. 'You may call me Anona, and you may ask me any question you wish.'

Tom was still puzzled and surprised by this encounter. It was nothing like he had imagined it would be. Princess Amathena had told him to expect a being of great beauty and great wisdom. The first half was correct, but where was the wisdom in playing such silly word games?

'Are you really the Sacred Anemone?' asked Tom.

'That's not a question, that's a doubt,' said Anona. 'Ask me another.'

'What was the point of that silly word game?'

'That's not a question, that's an opinion,' said Anona. 'Ask me another.'

'Are you really as old as the Princess said you are?'

'That's not a question, that's being nosey,' said Anona. 'Ask me another.'

'How long is this ridiculous conversation going to last?'

'That's not a question, that's being impatient,' said Anona. 'Ask me another.'

'When are you going to start answering my questions?'

'That's not a question, that's being stupid!' said Anona. 'You have not been listening to what I've been saying. I have been answering your questions, but not in the way you expected. I've been answering the deeper things that lie behind your questioning mind.'

Tom's mind raced in a million different directions. On the one hand he was aware of the urgency of the situation. The Crystal Sea was rapidly draining away and soon life for the little beach community would end. On the other hand, the Princess had told him that the secret plans for the rescue operation which would save the creatures of Crystalan could be found with the Sacred Anemone.

Apparently this beautiful yet unpredictable being had been given the high privilege of recording and storing the wisdom of the Rainchild.

'Please help me to understand,' pleaded Tom. 'I want to be useful and do something to save Crystalan, but I feel so weak and helpless.'

'It is not you who will save Crystalan,' replied Anona, 'indeed, you cannot, but you have been sent here to play an important part in restoring life to this lost world. You have already done much to help. You showed the Cosywags how to swim again and through this they discovered a lost art which has always been possible for them. You encouraged the creatures to burn their Gusters to demonstrate faith in the Rainchild and in their new-found ability to live under water. You have given new hope to the community by leading them into battle with Megagrit. And most of all, you have been willing to give of yourself in order to help others.'

'But the battle has not been won!' muttered Tom in despair.

'The battle must be won in your heart first, Tom,' said Anona, 'then we can go for THE BIG ONE!'

'What's "the big one"?' asked Tom.

'No more questions now, Tom. Learn from what has been said already and this will prepare you for the biggest event since our world was created. You will see the Rainchild!'

'I've already seen him in a picture on the wall of a cave.'

'Oh, that! Yes, I inscribed that picture myself when the cave was my home. I moved house when the waters subsided, but I plan to move back there one day!'

Anona paused as if savouring the moment when it would return home.

'You are going to see much more than a picture, Tom. You will see the Rainchild in person. In fact you have already seen him, but you did not recognise him. Soon it will become clear.'

The glittering colours sparkled with a greater intensity as Anona pondered the thought. Tom felt a sudden sense of exhilaration and excitement, the sort of feeling you get when you run down the beach and dive into the crashing waves of the oncoming sea. Nothing could stop them now!

'If the Rainchild is going to help us, then we can't lose!' shouted Tom.

'He's been helping you all the time, but you didn't realise it,' said Anona. 'Who do you think sent help when you fell over in the minefield? Who do you think made sure you would be safe when it seemed all was lost as you were sucked into the terrifying whirlpool? Who do you think helped you in the terrible battle with the Sandmen on the beach? Who kept you safe when you entered Megagrit's castle? And do you think it was luck that saved you when you were caught in mid-air as your basket hurtled towards the ground? You have been under the watchful eye of the Rainchild.'

'But what about Clarence and the other Cosywags who went down the Black Hole? They are dead; nobody saved them!'

'Is that what you think, Tom? You still have a lot to learn.'

Suddenly everything went dark, the bubble in which Tom had been sitting burst, and he found himself desperately thrashing about in the water trying to reach the surface. With the welcome help of the Cosywags, he pulled himself over the edge of the basket, still bobbing up and down in the shelter of the Hanging Rock, and slumped down in the middle, puffing and panting.

'Here,' said Clarissa, 'take some food and water. You must be starving.'

'Where did that come from?' said Tom with a note of relief in his voice.

'Slick flew back and dropped some provisions down for us. He said we may be here longer than we think but that we should not worry, because what had to be done, had to be done. Now tell us what happened,' continued Clarissa excitedly.

'I have been told that I have to win the battle in my heart,' said Tom slowly and thoughtfully. 'The Sacred Anemone didn't seem to answer my questions but then said that my questions had been answered in a deeper way.'

'Go on!' encouraged Clarissa.

'I asked if the creature was the Sacred Anemone and was told that this was not a question but a doubt.'

'You have been told to believe with all your heart,' said Clarissa.

'We played this silly word game and I asked what the point of it was. I was told that this was not a question but an opinion.'

'You have been told to discipline your mind to accept the illogical,' said Clarissa.

'I asked the Anemone if it really was as old as I had been led to believe and was told not to be nosey.'

'You have been told to see what the crucial issues are and not be sidetracked by minor things,' said Clarissa.

'I asked how long we were going to waste time with such a ridiculous conversation and was told I was being impatient.'

'You have been told to learn how to wait for the right moment rather than acting on impulse,' said Clarissa.

'The Anemone told me that I had seen the Rainchild without recognising him.'

'Don't be deceived by appearances, Tom,' said Clarissa, with a knowing look on her face. 'I thought you'd learned that lesson already!'

10

The Cosywags Keep a Promise

Tom was woken from a deep sleep by the wailing sound of the Jellybot. From where Tom was, in the basket moored underneath the Hanging Rock, it sounded like a ship's foghorn, although there was no fog on this bright, clear morning.

'Whatever is going on?' muttered Tom.

The Cosywags had gathered round him to tell him the news.

'The Jellybot is signalling to the Sacred Anemone. We believe he is indicating that the time has come for the liberation of Crystalan. But first he wants to make sure that you have received your instructions and are ready for THE BIG ONE.'

Tom looked puzzled. 'Why does everything always hinge on me? I need to see Anona before our visit is complete. I'm going to dive again to see if I can make further contact.'

The water looked cool and inviting and the sun, which had risen just an hour before, was beginning to shed a warm glow over everything. Tom dived into the water and made for the place where he had met the Sacred Anemone the night before. He didn't need to look far. Anona was emanating those bright dazzling colours again and the tiny shafts of laser light made the scene look like a highly advanced hi-tech concert event.

Sure enough, just as before, he suddenly found himself surrounded by the protective air bubble and he was free to talk and listen in an environment of total safety.

'Good morning, Tom,' said Anona. 'Sorry about the abrupt end to our conversation last night, but I felt that you had taken enough information for one sitting and needed to go away and think things through. Did you?'

'Yes, I did a lot of thinking last night, and I want to thank you for helping me to learn lessons about myself. I will never forget that phrase, "I know an anemone ..."'

Anona butted in, 'Yes, that's all very fine, but that was yesterday. This is a new day, with new objectives, new lessons to learn and new experiences to share!'

'Right!' said Tom eagerly. 'What's on the agenda for today?'

'Can you play chess?'

'Not very well, but I know how all the pieces move,' said Tom.

'Take a look at this.'

Tom nearly fell over backwards when, right in front of him, a chess board appeared with all the pieces placed on it as if a game was in progress. He reached out very gingerly to touch it, and his hand went straight through the board as if it were transparent.

'I can see it, but there's nothing there,' said Tom in bewilderment.

'I'm using electrical energy to create the form that you can see,' said Anona. 'Quite clever, don't you think? The idea of the game, as you know, is to trap the opponent's most important piece, the King. When there is no way out, and the King is cornered, the game is won. This is called "Check Mate".'

'But what am I supposed to learn from this?' asked Tom.

'Have you noticed the position of the pieces on the board? Sometimes it is necessary to sacrifice an important piece in order to win the game.'

As Tom looked at the board, it suddenly dawned on him what Anona was getting at. In order for the white pieces to capture the black King, thus winning the game, they would first have to allow their white Queen to be taken.

'Princess Amathena!' said Tom. 'Megagrit was allowed to take her!'

'Precisely,' responded Anona.

'But what has that achieved?' spluttered Tom, trying to keep calm.

'Megagrit believes that by holding the princess he will force a showdown with the Rainchild and that this will result in his ultimate takeover of power. He is living in a fantasy world, though, because he can never win.'

'So what will the Rainchild do?' asked Tom with urgency in his voice.

'He is going to save our world in a way that Megagrit could never imagine or anticipate, and we are going to witness this amazing event. It will surely be THE BIG ONE we have all been waiting for.'

'When will this event happen?'

'The Jellybot has been communicating with me

this morning. The event has already begun and will be finished in twenty-four hours,' said Anona.

'But what about the princess?'

'She gave herself up, freely knowing the dangers involved. I can tell you, though, that no harm will come to her.'

'And what part do I play in all this?'

'You are already playing your part. And there are greater things in store for you in the future. You are being allowed to see things that have never been seen before, to experience things that have never been experienced before, to hear things that have never been heard before, and to know things that have never been known before.'

Tom sat still with his mouth wide open.

'Whenever you are in the land of Crystalan, you will be our witness and messenger. We needed someone we could trust to tell our story. You've passed the test!'

'Messenger?' exclaimed Tom with surprise.

'Yes, Tom, you have been chosen to hold the pictures you have seen, the experiences you have had and the lessons you have learned, so that our world will never forget this day. Whenever you face a problem or have a question, you can always find guidance from me. Every one of the hundreds of thousands of tentacles I am equipped with, carry memory banks full of information that can be acquired by those who know the secret code.'

'And what is that?' asked Tom, still dazed from being told he was to be a special 'messenger'.

'You already know it, Tom. It is revealed only to those whose heart is ready and whose motives are pure.'

Tom knew immediately what he was talking

about. 'So it wasn't a pointless tongue twister after all!' he said '"I know an anemone named Anona!" Yes, pretty ingenious, that one!'

'Whenever you utter these words in sincerity, you will receive the wisdom you desire. Now you have to get back to the beach. There is a lot of activity going on there right at this very moment. I wouldn't want you to miss out. Remember that whatever problem befalls you, you will always be given a way out.'

Tom was ready for it this time. The bubble burst and he pushed his way to the surface of the water and round to where the basket was moored. After telling Clarissa and the others what had happened, he called to the Hummingbats who were sitting on top of the rock. They dutifully lowered the golden rope which was attached to the ring, and with their strong transparent wings burring away like small engines, they lifted the basket with its occupants. Within twenty minutes they were back on the beach.

Anona was right: something was brewing.

There was a huddle of Cosywags standing round the Jellybot listening intently to some instructions he was giving them. As they came away they were carrying small containers of a greenish, bluish liquid that seemed to have smoke coming from them. They were being very careful with the substance, making sure not to spill any or get any on their bodies.

Further along the beach there was a line of Clawhammers lying down side by side, including Brutus and Bruno, with their heads propped up on makeshift pillows made out of the green foliage from the beach.

'What's going on?' enquired Tom.

Clarissa volunteered the answer. 'The Cosywags are keeping a promise they made to the Clawhammers at the time when they rescued you from the Black Hole. The Cosywags are bathing their heads to arrest the progress of the Cankor disease. This will ease the pain and stop any further decay. I notice that they have been given some special instructions from the Jellybot.'

They walked over to watch this amazing sight.

Tom couldn't help remembering one of the first things he saw when entering this world: Clarence the Cosywag being swung round by his tail by that old bully Brutus. How much had changed in such a short time, he thought. There seemed to be a new friendship and sense of unity that had not been there before.

The Clawhammers were obviously in pain, but as the Cosywags knelt over them and gently applied the solution to their heads, it was clear that the acute pain was being relieved and the soreness alleviated.

As this little ceremony was going on, another group of Cosywags started singing a soft and gentle chant making a slow steady rhythm as they sang. They were using drum-like instruments made out of leaves stretched over bamboo canes and some carried bells and rattles. As they sang they danced in unison.

'Boom, ta ta ta, Boom, ta ta ta' went the rhythm.

> Drops of rain, drops of rain,
> Bring your healing once again.
> Send your light, send your light,
> Into the darkness of our night.
> Bring us back into the glory,

Of the former wonder story.
Rainchild come and set us free.
Let us all your mercy see.

The chanting and singing went on and there was an air of celebration and anticipation all around, a kind of peaceful acceptance that all would be well.

Clive and Clarissa were standing together with Tom when suddenly they felt drops of water falling on their faces. They looked up and saw an amazing sight. Hovering over them was the Golden Cloud, like a massive floating castle of fluffy gold, with beautiful contoured shapes radiating a shimmering golden haze all around it. Tom noticed that the cloud did not block out the light of the sun, but rather outshone it, creating a bright golden glow over the land. Big drops of rain were gently falling to the ground from the cloud and each one reflected the colours of the rainbow as it fell.

As the rain touched the faces of the creatures, who by now were all looking up in wonder and awe, a transformation took place. Tom felt a tingling feeling all over his body as the raindrops touched him.

Excited squeals rose up from a group of Cosywags and suddenly everyone was aware of the fact that the Clawhammers were no longer lying on their backs in agony, but were standing, with arms stretched wide and faces looking up in deep thankfulness. The raindrops had completely restored their bodies and every trace of the Cankor disease was gone!

So much excitement filled the air, that no one noticed the Jellybot moving.

With a slow, deliberate shuffle, the huge mass started to turn towards the Crystal Sea, now at least a hundred metres away. Tom estimated that the waters were pulling back from the beach at the rate of one metre each hour and that this process was speeding up as the combination of acute evaporation, plus the rapid draining of water through the Black Hole, took its effect.

Clive and Clarissa had no idea what was going on behind them, until they felt the ground vibrating as the Jellybot heaved its huge body over the sand.

'Don't move any further!' shouted Clarissa in obvious panic. 'Don't forget the minefield, it's still active. You'll never make it through!'

Clive grabbed Clarissa's paw and they started running towards the Jellybot.

'Don't worry,' he shouted, squeezing her paw tighter with every step, 'Brutus personally supervised the dismantling of the minefield when they arrived back last evening. He was so grateful for what you and the others did for him and his brother.'

They reached the Jellybot, Tom arriving a few seconds later. Although they were still out of breath, the words of concern came flooding out.

'What are you doing? You won't survive such dangerous antics! You are not designed to move on land! You will do yourself damage that can never be repaired!'

The Jellybot looked straight at them, his big eyes looking tired, yet with a sense of satisfaction.

'The raindrops are giving me energy,' he said quietly and confidently, 'and I have done all I can do here on the beach. I must now go on to fulfil my mission.'

By now a crowd had gathered, all looking concerned and anxious for the welfare of the Jellybot. He had become an indispensable part of life for the small community, always there to give advice and help, and always seeming to know exactly what they were thinking. Even though the Clawhammers had ridiculed him and the evil Sandmen had hurt him badly by hurling rocks and grit at him on the terrible day of the battle, he still seemed to stay calm and caring.

It was then that Tom began to wonder about something that had never occurred to him before. Why had Megagrit been so concerned to make sure that the Jellybot could not reach the Crystal Sea? He had given orders for the minefield to be sown and the Clawhammers, under his evil control, had carried out those orders. But why take so much trouble over one harmless Jellybot?

'I know what you are thinking, Tom,' said the Jellybot. 'You have learned so much since coming to Crystalan, so I think you know the reason why I must reach the waters.'

'Yes, I think I do know,' said Tom, seriously. 'I'll do all I can to help.'

The rain had stopped falling now and the Golden Cloud had moved out of sight. As its glow departed a sense of eeriness came over the beach, and everyone began to cling to one another automatically as if expecting some terrible tragedy to take place.

'I must keep moving,' said the Jellybot. 'Remember: whatever happens, trust the Rainchild.'

A yellowy mist began swirling over the beach and for a moment it was difficult to see more than a few metres away. Tom felt very uneasy, and even though the heat of the sun penetrated through the mist, a cold shiver went up his back. Everyone stood still and the only sound that could be heard was the slow, deliberate movement of the Jellybot on his determined shuffle towards the sea.

'I think there is a sandstorm blowing up,' said Clarissa, clutching Tom's hand. 'We haven't seen anything like this since the day the Jellybot arrived.'

'So the Jellybot must have lost his way and was grounded in the storm. When the waters subsided he was left high and dry,' said Tom, with a questioning tone in his voice.

'That's how the story goes,' said Clarissa, 'but no one really knows. We couldn't see anything because of the storm. We are sure that the evil Megagrit makes it happen in some way. It's strange that we haven't seen anything like this since that day. It's almost as if something terrible is about to take place.'

'Or something marvellous,' said Tom gently.

Clarissa began to weep. Great tears rolled down her cheek and fell onto the ground.

'Don't cry,' said Clive. 'Remember what the Jellybot said. Whatever happens, we must go on trusting the Rainchild.'

A huge rumble of evil laughter shook the beach.

Sand started flying everywhere, and Tom had to cover his face with his hands to protect himself from the impact of the tiny bits of grit shooting like bullets all around. The wind was so strong that he was knocked off his feet and he went skidding and bumping over the beach towards the cliff face.

Above the howl of the wind and the cutting impact of the sandstorm, Tom heard the unmistakable voice of Megagrit like a nightmare that would not go away.

'Rainchild! Listen to my voice! I will not allow you to win! See the damage I am causing to your precious Crystalan! Give yourself to me and I will stop this raging storm! Prove your love for the creatures by ending their misery! I will not allow you to reach the Crystal Sea!'

11

The Surprise Attack

Since his audience with Anona the Sacred Anemone, Tom had suspected this: now he thought it was almost certainly true.

Confirmation had come in the most unexpected way, through the angry and violent words of evil Megagrit. There was more to the Jellybot than met the eye.

Tom was pinned against the rock face by the force of the sandstorm — not a very healthy position to be in! There was no time to make intricate plans; quick decisions were needed.

Tom had been in tight spots on several occasions during the last few eventful days, but this one seemed to top the lot!

It was almost impossible to see what was going on around the beach, and he wondered how the Jellybot was faring in his attempt to reach the Crystal Sea. He dreaded to think what might be the outcome should he fail to do so.

Tom could really feel the adrenalin moving now as with all the strength he could muster, he groped his way along the cliff face, feeling that he must surely be very near to the spot where they had erected the basket and pulley system up the side of the cliff. If only he could grab one of the ropes, there was a chance he could get to the cave and then to the top of the cliff to find out exactly what was going on up there. He had come so far: he would not accept defeat now, Megagrit or no Megagrit.

With one hand protecting his eyes from the blast of the sand and the other reaching out into the air in front of him, he gradually made his way along the beach by the edge of the cliff. Above the howl of the wind, he could hear what must be the basket knocking wildly against the cliff face. While he was still trying to find the rope with one hand, the breath was suddenly knocked out of him by the basket hitting him in the stomach. He fell dazed and winded to the ground as pain shot through his body.

Tom knew that the basket would be swinging over his head, so he was careful not to stand in its path, but reached up carefully with his hand ready to grab hold of it. He felt it brush past his hand at speed and got ready for the swing back to make an attempt to get it. He felt it a second time and hung on for all he was worth to the cane rim running around the bottom.

The chances of him being able to hold and control the basket in such a storm were a million to one. Tom quietly thanked the Rainchild for once again helping him to achieve the near impossible.

He soon found himself scrambling over the side of the basket and falling inside where there was some protection from the rush of the wind and sand. With the extra weight inside, the basket was more stable, and gave Tom a few seconds' breathing space. He summoned his energy for the immense effort needed to haul himself up the rope.

The wind seemed to be getting stronger, and the sandstorm more violent by the second. Tom could hear the voice of Megagrit still booming out threatening words aimed at the Jellybot.

'Why do you persist in your pointless quest for the waters of the Crystal Sea? Soon there will be no water and you will die! Give me your allegiance and I will ensure that you survive in comfort with these insignificant little creatures of yours!'

From what he knew of Megagrit all his promises were useless, and in any case life without the refreshing qualities of the Crystal Sea would be pointless.

Collections of sand were building up in the basket blown in by the irregular wind currents, and there were also glittering silver bits mixed in with the pile which made Tom dismiss all thoughts of moving for at least another minute.

'The silvery freedom dust,' he muttered to himself. 'The deposits washed up on the beach are also being blown around together with the sand. "Remember that whatever problems befall you, you will always be given a way out!"' The wise words of Anona came flooding back into his mind. 'Yes, of course! Answers to problems are wound up in the problems themselves. What we need to do is discover how to unravel the answers!'

Tom couldn't help thinking that if anyone heard him muttering to himself, they would have thought he had gone completely mad!

'At long last I'm coming to my senses,' he shouted. 'Watch out, Megagrit, I'm on my way!'

With a new strength and resolve, he reached up and grabbed the rope that was attached to the top of the basket and began hauling himself upwards. The silvery dust whizzing past his ears would not be a substitute for effort on his part, but it would certainly give an extra degree of safety to an extremely hazardous operation. The dust had certainly released a new power and determination in Tom as he began his gruelling climb.

Suddenly he felt the rope jerk, and he began moving gently towards his goal. He looked down to see who was working the pulley, but visibility was so poor he couldn't see more than a metre below him.

It was a little tricky getting from the rope into the cave mouth but he managed to do it by jumping into the second basket which was at the top of the pulley, and from there he scrambled into the virtual peace of the cave.

He stood up and looked down towards the beach. He was above the sandstorm now, but just a metre below him the storm stretched out, looking like a violent, rolling sea. He reflected on the utter contrast of life according to Megagrit and the life offered by the Rainchild. Here was a perfect illustration before his own eyes. One offered a sea of violence, aggression and death, and the other a sea of peace, vitality and beauty.

Obviously Megagrit was not aware of the existence of the cave, for the pictures on the wall were still intact. Tom made his way respectfully past them and up towards the exit at the back. He knew this would bring him on to the top of the cliff to face whatever was there.

He noticed some large stone jars tucked over to one side, and on investigation discovered that they were full of the silver dust. The Cosywags must have stored the dust to ensure that plenty of supplies would be available in case of emergency. He grabbed a few handfuls and stuffed it into his trouser pockets.

Crawling out through the hole in the back of the cave, he had a good look around him, making sure that the rocks surrounding the hole gave him adequate cover to avoid being detected. Even though he half expected it, he was still shocked when he saw what was going on.

There was Megagrit, looking twice as big as he was before, towering over the edge of the cliff looking down on the sandstorm. The journey across the desert had accumulated lots of bits and pieces of gravel and dirt, stuck to his body in ugly shapes. There were at least thirty-five Sandmen standing all around, and eight of them were carrying the smoking cauldron which had occupied pride of place by the side of Megagrit in his castle audience room. They held it high on two long poles that were slotted through the handles on the sides.

An incredible noise of clanging and whirring machinery distracted Tom from this ugly sight, and he became aware of what was causing the terrible storm. On each side of Megagrit was a gigantic wind machine. The machines were operated by several of the Sandmen who were dwarfed by the size of the massive propellers.

Megagrit screamed orders at them.

'More power! More power! Make those creatures pay! All of you, look and see who is in control now!'

Tom had an irresistible urge to run forward and push Megagrit over the edge, but he realised immediately the futility of such an act. The bulk of that evil being was so huge that it would be like colliding with a brick wall, and he would not be able to move him one centimetre.

Over to the left of him there was a long line of Sandmen waiting in a queue. He glanced down to the first in line who was being covered by a substance being taken out of the cauldron. It looked like paste, only when it had been applied to their bodies, it was glittering and shimmering like a sequin suit. He looked back at Megagrit and the Sandmen controlling the wind machines and they too had this strange silvery appearance.

This puzzling sight worried Tom.

Thinking quickly, he grabbed a large stone and threw it as hard as he could at one of the huge wind machines. It missed completely and disappeared out of sight over the edge of the cliff. With all the activity going on, no one noticed the stone flying through the air. Tom had a sudden fear that perhaps it had hit somebody down below. He must not miss a second time.

He crawled out from the protection of his rock and moved nearer to the machine. Picking up a second stone he took careful aim and threw it. This time it struck the spinning propeller, but instead of the desired effect of jamming the mechanism, the machine simply cut the stone into pieces and tiny bits ricocheted off in all directions like bullets.

One bit struck Megagrit in the side and he let out a deep groan. There followed a long silence.

It seemed to Tom as if everything had been

stopped like a freeze frame on a video playback machine. Could things really go badly wrong at this stage in the proceedings? Like a recurring bad dream, these encounters with Megagrit seemed never ending.

Realising his moment of surprise was gone, he jumped up and started sprinting towards the lever operating one of the wind machines. Diving into the air, he grabbed it with both hands, at the same time swinging and kicking his legs out at an approaching Sandman. Tom was surprised to see him stagger backwards into his comrade who was also knocked off balance. The weight of his body pulled the lever down and the machine slowly stopped.

He released his grip and fell to the ground, landing on his feet. He started sprinting towards the second machine.

By this time there seemed to be organised chaos! One of the Sandmen was shouting orders at the others who were now forming up around the second machine ready to face the onslaught of this young determined boy running at them. The group in the queue dispersed and joined in the activity. Half of them were covered in the shimmering paste, and half of them looked normal. Well, as normal as you can be expected to look if you are a Sandman.

Megagrit did not move. Still facing out over the sandstorm, which was raging furiously even though one of the wind machines had been stopped, he seemed to have no concern about the frantic goings on behind him.

Tom realised he stood no chance of getting through to switch off this second machine with all those bodies in the way, so he stopped in his tracks. Right at his feet was another small rock. He picked it up, swung it back to the side of him, just as he always did when skimming stones across the top of the water, then let it go. It went hurtling like a frisbee towards the propeller of the second machine.

In unison, all the Sandmen turned to see what would happen as the rock zoomed over their heads.

At the very same moment, when every eye was on the flying rock, Tom started sprinting straight towards Megagrit.

Unprotected and unguarded, he seemed to be an easy target.

All the effort required was wasted energy. When the collision came, it was Tom that came off worse.

Much worse.

He was knocked painfully to the ground by more flying bits of rock that had been smashed by the propeller in the same way as before. Megagrit did not even flinch at the impact and indeed did not seem to notice anything out of order.

Tom came to after a few seconds and took a quick look round. Several of the Sandmen who had been standing around the second wind machine were moaning and wandering around in a daze with their hands over their faces. Some of the bits of rock had obviously hit the Sandmen in the eyes.

He looked up at the towering bulk of Megagrit, and then realised what the sequin suit was all about. He was covered with a paste which was full of the silvery freedom dust. This must have come from the supplies delivered to him by the Clawhammers before their change of heart.

As the Jellybot had once explained, in the hands

of evil, the dust had the reverse effect. Instead of supporting freedom, goodness and peace, it reflected the heart of the user and became an agent of destruction. Tom found it hard to believe that such a fantastic gift from the Rainchild could ever be used and abused so as to advance evil. Megagrit was using the dust as personal protection against any attack with water. It had created an impenetrable suit of armour that nothing could get through.

No wonder Megagrit was so confident.

Suddenly Tom heard a voice he recognised.

'Please don't do anything foolish, Tom! You can't do this alone! Get away now while you have a chance to escape!'

'Princess Amathena!' Tom whispered to himself. He jumped to his feet. 'Where are you? I want to help!'

'I'm over here,' she said.

Tom glanced around quickly, and saw that the princess was standing in a large stone receptacle rather like a telephone box. It had bars on one side and four large stone wheels, one on each corner. It was standing on its own in a clearing near where the queue had been.

He grabbed a handful of the freedom dust from one of his pockets, and ran over to the cage. Nobody seemed to worry too much about his frantic activity. Nobody moved to intercept him or prevent him getting to the princess.

She was still as beautiful as Tom had remembered, and even though she was confined in a cruel and humiliating way she did not show any signs of hatred or fear.

'That won't help,' she said, pointing to the handful of dust in his hand.

'But I can't let you stay in that prison. There must be a better way!'

'The only way is to follow the wisdom of the Rainchild,' she said.

'How can this be wisdom, when you are being treated like this?'

Tom threw the dust at the cage expecting it to be broken open and bring release to the princess. Instead there was a series of cracking noises like the sound of a whip, and the dust was repelled away from the cage in a burst of bright lights like tiny lightning flashes.

'The cage has a protective coating of the dust paste,' said the princess. 'Megagrit and many of the Sandmen have the same protection.'

'It's not fair!' screamed Tom indignantly.

At that moment the silence was broken by the rumbling voice of Megagrit himself.

'Hello, Tom, I've been expecting you,' he said, slowly turning round.

Tom remembered hearing that phrase several times already but in much more pleasant circumstances. Everybody seemed to have been expecting him as if he was part of some fantastic plan. The voice seemed to be much more mellow and less threatening.

'Without knowing it, you have stepped into the biggest opportunity of your young life. The battle with the Rainchild is nearly over, and I will be recognised as the ruler of Crystalan.'

Tom turned to face Megagrit. He was aware that he was surrounded by Sandmen.

Megagrit continued. 'You could rule with me, Tom. With your speed and courage and my brains and power, we could create a world of our making without interference from imposters and do-gooders. All will bow down in fear to us, the greatest force of all time! Join me now, Tom, it's your only hope!'

His voice reached a crescendo like a sonic boom and all the Sandmen started shaking uncontrollably as if shivering in a cold wind.

There was silence for at least a minute. The atmosphere was electric, everyone wondering what would happen next.

'I will do as you say on one condition,' said Tom slowly and thoughtfully.

'What is that?' asked Megagrit, composing himself.

'Give me Princess Amathena.'

A clanging noise filled the air as the bars of the cage fell away.

'She's yours,' replied Megagrit, with a look of final triumph on his face.

12

Here Comes the Flood

Tom swung round and stared at the empty cage.

'Where is she?' he demanded.

Megagrit laughed. 'You don't think I'd risk her life by bringing her into this war zone, do you?'

'But I saw her with my own eyes!' shrieked Tom.

'A little trick with an electrical force field,' said Megagrit. 'That Sacred Anemone of yours is not the only one who can perform miracles you know!'

'You said I could have the Princess,' said Tom, a little bewildered.

'And so you shall, but first you must help me bring this little battle to a successful conclusion.'

For the first time that he could ever remember. Tom felt that he was being pulled in two opposite directions at the same time, and it was very painful.

Tom started chanting the formula to get access to the wisdom of the Sacred Anemone.

'I know an anemone named Anona. I know an

anemone named Anona. I know an anemone named Anona.' The events of the last few days flashed through his mind, then suddenly there was no longer a fight going on inside him; he knew exactly what he must do.

'What's that you're babbling about?' demanded Megagrit.

'You are about to see who the real boss is around here,' shouted Tom.

He felt a strange sense of calm as with all the strength he could muster, he started sprinting towards the edge of the cliff.

Megagrit had a look of amusement on his face, which quickly turned to disbelief, as Tom hurtled over the side of the cliff and down into the raging sandstorm and certain death below.

With a feeling of elation, Tom stretched his arms wide as he fell, as if embracing the storm. He hit the billowing clouds of sand and lost all sense of direction as he continued his deadly journey down to the beach.

It all happened in a few seconds, but Tom distinctly felt as if he were being cushioned from underneath. He later learned that this was the effect of the silvery dust being blown about with the sand.

He felt a gentle impact on landing and then the sensation of sliding on a rather familiar surface.

'Hello, Tom,' said the Jellybot with a glint in his eye. 'I've been expecting you! You're just in time to see the completion of the plan to bring life back to our world. By the way, please don't grab my eyelashes this time, it was extremely painful the first time round!'

Tom was sitting astride the Jellybot's nose and looking him straight in the eye as the Jellybot made his way across the beach to the water. Words failed Tom for a moment, so the Jellybot continued. 'Never again make bargains with the enemy, Tom, it can never work.'

'But I never intended to go along with it,' protested Tom.

'Using deception and dishonesty are the marks of evil,' said the Jellybot. 'Have nothing to do with them and you will live at peace with yourself.'

The Jellybot waded through the shallows of the water, and continued speaking as he gradually moved into deeper waters.

'All the creatures are safe,' he said. 'I instructed them all to make for the water and dive into the calm and safety of the sea. There is only one missing.'

'Who is that?' asked Tom anxiously.

'Brutus insisted on going back to the top of the beach to help you.'

'Of course. It must have been him working the pulley system to get me up to the cave entrance. I knew somebody was there. I must go back to help!'

Tom slid down into the shallow water and, splashing towards the beach, fought his way through the biting sand towards the pulley controls by the cliff face. He finally reached the point and searched round frantically to find Brutus. No one was in sight.

Then, without warning, he tripped over a huge lump in the sand. Reaching down, he quickly brushed the sand away as best he could, and there, lying motionless, was Brutus.

The sand had completely buried him.

'Brutus! Brutus! Wake up!' shouted Tom in a panic. 'You can't die! Wake up!'

Brutus felt tears fall onto his face as Tom bent over him sobbing. Slowly he managed to move his lips and spoke in urgent whispered tones.

'Get me to the water! We both need to get to the water!'

Tom scrambled down and grabbed Brutus by his feet. He tried desperately to haul him across the beach. He thought that his lungs might explode at any minute with the amount of effort he was putting in.

Painfully and slowly, he dragged the helpless body towards the water. Although the flying sand continued to sting as it hit their bodies, at least it provided a dust cover which made them invisible to Megagrit.

By now the Jellybot was fully immersed and moving gracefully and majestically out into the sea. He knew his destiny and headed straight for the Black Hole.

All the Cosywags, including Clarissa and Clive, were forming an escort for him but nobody was smiling for they all knew the terrible price he was about to pay.

Only he could save Crystalan and the moment had come.

As the procession swam deeper into the waters, they passed the Hanging Rock. Dazzling bright colours were streaming out in all directions as Anona acknowledged that now was the time. Its tentacles waved backwards and forwards like a sea of hands at a football match cheering the winning team.

None of those accompanying the Jellybot felt that what was about to happen could be described as 'winning', rather it was a necessary sacrifice and an amazing act of love.

Slick and the other Slickwingers flew over the water, watching the Jellybot and his escort as they moved through the transparent water. The big birds and the Hummingbats had been grounded during the storm, but now they glowed with pride as they anticipated the big moment.

Tom stopped in his struggle to move Brutus and looked around him. The sandstorm was dying down. The beach was covered in sand dunes; everything else had gone. He looked around hoping to see the Jellybot, but he was nowhere to be seen.

Brutus started moving slightly and after a few moments managed to prop himself up on his elbows. He looked dazed and wounded, but not critically. Tom dropped both his legs and rushed round, grabbing him by the shoulders and giving him a big hug.

'Ouch!' yelled Brutus.

'Oops! Sorry about the legs,' said Tom. 'I'm so glad you are still with us.'

'Only the good die young!' said Brutus with a sparkle in his eye.

Tom didn't say it, but he thought that was definitely another one of those stupid meaningless sayings that people use when they can't think of anything else to say.

'Look!' exclaimed Brutus, pointing up over the sea. 'There's the Golden Cloud!'

He struggled to get to his feet. 'Quick,' he said, 'we cannot afford to lose one moment. It is time for you to go back into your own world.'

'But what about Megagrit? What about Princess Amathena? What about the Purple Plug?'

'No time for questions now,' shouted Brutus. 'Follow me!'

At first he started plodding along the beach towards the sea, then he broke into a steady jog and then a fast run. Tom was surprised how fast a Clawhammer could move considering the weight of its body, but he managed to keep up, just about.

He thought there must be something very serious about to happen to make Brutus move so fast. What was all that about going back home?

Tom had a sudden urge to stop and look back.

'Don't look back,' warned Brutus, running on ahead. 'The sight will distract you!'

It was too late.

Tom stood mesmerised as if locked in a magnetic field that was pulling him irresistibly towards its source. His feet were operating against his will with robot-like movements, and his whole body was swaying mechanically as if under remote control. He tried to shout for help but his lips would not move.

Stretched along the top of the cliff were the evil Megagrit and his Sandmen.

They looked out over the sea, forming a sinister audience to the proceedings about to take place. Megagrit was still shouting out words of abuse aimed at the Rainchild and his followers, and the sequin effect which covered their bodies gave them a strangely attractive appearance. The form of the Princess Amathena could be clearly seen standing next to Megagrit — a tragic picture of innocence in the presence of evil.

Brutus, realising that Tom was no longer behind him, stopped in his tracks. He started walking backwards, determined not to be drawn by the sight of Megagrit. He took each step extremely carefully, calling out Tom's name as he went. The sun was high over the cliff behind, so he looked out for the shadow of Tom's body on the sand.

'Hold on, Tom. I'm coming to help. Don't give in. Resist the temptation. You have the power to win!'

As soon as he saw the shadow, he reached back with his clawed hands until he touched Tom. Then, tightly closing his eyes, he quickly turned and put both hands over Tom's eyes, at the same time whispering gently in his ear, 'You belong to the Rainchild now! You belong to the Rainchild now! Have no fear, be at peace.'

He swung Tom round and gently lifted him on to his strong shoulders. Then he jogged towards the water.

He ran straight in and ducked Tom under, covering him from top to toe. The soothing quality and refreshing vitality of the water released Tom from the trance he had been in and he quickly recovered his senses.

Meanwhile, the Jellybot and entourage had reached their chosen destination: the edge of the whirlpool. Everyone stopped in the water and listened to the Jellybot speak.

'We have been through some exciting, frightening and at times dangerous adventures. Since I have been with you on the beach, we have watched the waters of the Crystal Sea gradually diminishing, taking with them all hope of life. Many of you got used to living without the water, but as a consequence your lives were empty, without purpose and sadly limited. Some of you suffered serious diseases and have been at the point of death. Even though your traditions stretch back many hundreds of years, the old ways were forgotten. You have learned many hard lessons. But you have rediscovered your heritage now and are beginning to live again in fullness.'

The only sound was that of the moving currents of water, finding their way through the beautiful rock formations all around. Even the abundant forests of weed seemed to be still, listening to words that everyone recognised were coming from the Rainchild himself.

'Some of you still have not recognised who I am. My unsightly and cumbersome form fooled you into thinking I was a helpless creature to be pitied. But many have listened to my words spoken out loud, or uttered softly on the wind, and you discovered the key which unlocked the door to many miracles.'

The Jellybot began shifting position in the water, as if getting ready for the final act.

'I do this freely, for the sake of Crystalan,' he said. These were his last words, as with an awkward undignified movement, he up-ended himself, and slowly sank into the whirlpool.

'What's happening out there?' asked Tom.

'The Jellybot is giving his life by sacrificing himself to the Black Hole.'

'But there is no grid on it now; they moved it when they rescued me.'

'He knows that,' said Brutus. 'It was all part of the plan. He is giving his own body to take the place of the Purple Plug. The waters of the Crystal Sea will flow freely again and life will flourish.'

'But why doesn't the Rainchild help?' said Tom, still not fully recognising what was going on.

'The Jellybot *is* the Rainchild,' said Brutus slowly. 'He took on a different form in order to get alongside us and guide us to the answers to age-old problems. We are witnessing an incredible and unique act of love.'

The waters began to be agitated and the currents circling round their legs were becoming stronger.

'Quick,' said Brutus, 'get on my back. I am going to take you to the Black Hole. Please don't ask any more questions, just do as I ask.'

Tom scrambled onto the back of Brutus and he held on tightly round his muscular neck.

'Your way out of Crystalan and back to your home is through the Black Hole. The Jellybot will wait for you before he finally gives his life and fills the hole. Go straight through and don't turn back, otherwise you may never see your family again.'

Brutus was trying to hold back the tears. 'Thank you for all you have done for us, Tom. I hope we meet again.'

Brutus swam fast through the water and displayed his superior strength as he carried Tom with ease towards the Black Hole. He did not go under the water for he knew Tom could not survive such a trip.

When they got near to the whirlpool Brutus shouted to Tom, 'Take a deep breath, I'm going to take you under. Don't let go of me until I give you the word.'

They dived under the water and circled the area where the whirlpool was still rushing frantically downward. The Jellybot was within three metres of the Black Hole and was motionless in the water. Even the tremendous force of the whirlpool could not move him. He was waiting for Tom to make his escape.

Tom was scared. Surely this must mean death for him — and yet he was going willingly with a total trust in this unwieldy creature, Brutus the Clawhammer. He thought he must be going mad. Mind you, he had done some pretty crazy things in the last few days!

Brutus waved his arm. This was the sign that Tom was waiting for.

He let go of Brutus and before he could think straight he was caught in the downward rush of water. As he disappeared through the gaping hole, the Jellybot moved down and allowed his body to form the shape that the Purple Plug had once occupied, closing the gap and stopping the flow of escaping water.

Megagrit, still watching from the top of the cliff, turned, and with terror in his eyes headed back towards his castle in the desert.

If Tom had been on the surface of the water, he would have witnessed a unique and beautiful sight.

As the Jellybot died, crushed by the pressure of the water, onlookers could clearly see a vision of the Rainchild, rising out of the waters and moving majestically through the air and up to the Golden Cloud above. At the same time, hundreds of transparent air bubbles rose to the surface of the sea and then floated up through the air. There was a sudden burst of light as each bubble opened, creating a firework display of rainbow colours, while a silvery cascade of dust crystals came falling down to earth.

As the Rainchild reached the Golden Cloud there was a spontaneous burst of praise, as Clive and Clarissa, Brutus, Bruno and Slick, together with all the other creatures, raised their arms high at the joy of what they had seen.

The sea rose higher and higher. Soon it had risen up the beach and above the level of the cave and in the space of a few short hours, was running over the top of the cliff and down into the dry barren desert, bringing life wherever it went.

'Tom! If you don't come right now your tea will be cold!'

The voice of his mother was unmistakable. Tom found himself standing in the bathroom looking into the bath. The water was draining away in a clockwise motion through the plughole.

'That's the way it should be,' muttered Tom to himself.

He called down the stairs to his mother. 'Mum, how long have I been away?'

'What do you mean, "been away"? Have you gone crazy? You've been in the bathroom far too long, that's for sure. Your brother is taking his girlfriend out tonight and he's been waiting to get in there for at least fifteen minutes. Now, come down for your dinner at once!'

Tom walked into his bedroom. Everything looked the same. His mind was racing like a cassette player on fast forward.

'Only been away fifteen minutes,' he thought. 'It must have been some sort of a dream.'

Then he had a mind-boggling thought. He had come through the Black Hole. But so had Clarence and several of the Cosywags near the start of his adventure.

He rushed back into the bathroom, and there, poking out from underneath a hanging towel, were five pairs of paws. He snatched the towel away and to his utter amazement, there was Clarence and the others, safe and sound!

He lovingly picked them all up in his arms and tip-toed into his bedroom, whispering 'Hello' to them all. It was a good job that the trap door to the attic was in his room. That way he could hide his little friends and make sure they would not be disturbed.

After getting them safely installed, he changed his trousers. A pile of silvery dust dropped from his pockets onto the floor.

His mind was still working overtime.

'What happened to Megagrit? Was Princess Amathena rescued from his evil clutches? How were all his friends getting on in their new-found freedom? Would he ever see them again?'

That would be another story ....

Children Of The Voice

by Ishmael

He was Little Trouble by name, because the grown-ups who ruled Oldchurch thought he must be that by nature. Keep the Littlehorrors out of Real Church, and, when they show signs of growing up, leave them to the Bigwideworld.

But Little Trouble wants to hear the Voice—the One everyone says they go to church for. Fed up with Oldchurch, he sets off on his quest, passing on his way through Crosscountry, Wastetime University and the alluring Securicity.

He has a lot to learn, some new friends to make, and some surprising enemies. And at the end of it all, he has to go back to Oldchurch...

This is Ishmael's first work of fiction, blending the mood of *Pilgrim's Progress* and *Animal Farm*. Fun for any age, it speaks volumes about the divisions we so often try to maintain between God's older children and his younger ones.

Also by Ishmael in Kingsway paperback: *The History of Ishmael Part One* and *Angels with Dirty Faces*.

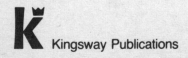

Kingsway Publications

The Book And The Phoenix

by Cherith Baldry

Times are hard for most of the Six Worlds. Earth is long forgotten, left behind in a past age when technology brought men and women to the stars.

The old tales tell how, generations ago, the colonists brought with them a belief, a faith, a way of life. But that's almost forgotten now, just a dream for old men.

Until now. Young Cradoc will see a vision of the legendary phoenix that will lead him to a Book. It is only when he discovers the power in the Book that he also learns there are many who will want to destroy it—and anyone who attempts to protect it.

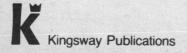
Kingsway Publications

Hostage Of The Sea

by Cherith Baldry

They came from over the sea, a nation of warriors intent on spreading their empire. When they descended upon a small kingdom that served the God of peace, the battle was short. And Aurion, the peaceful King's son, was the ideal hostage to secure victory.

Coming to the fearsome land of Tar-Askar, Aurion meets the strong and proud son of the warrior king. A most unlikely friendship develops—a bond of love that will prove a greater threat to the Tar-Askan empire than the weapons of war.

Also by **CHERITH BALDRY** in the *Stories of the Six Worlds: The Book and the Phoenix.*

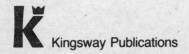

Kingsway Publications

The Muselings

by Ed Wicke

One day three scruffy children from an orphanage in the country have a surprise. Rachel, Robert and Alice fall *up* a tree into another world!

Why have they been brought into the land that scheming Queen Jess calls her own? The Queen and the children would *both* like to know, and as they try to find out, they stumble into hilarious and hair-raising adventures. Here we meet Lord Lrans, mad on hunting; the Reverend Elias, beloved but misunderstood vicar; Ballbody, a round, bouncy fellow...and the Muselings—kind, furry creatures whose world the children have fallen into.

Then Elias faces Queen Jess on a hilltop, and everything changes.

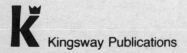

Kingsway Publications

The Will Of Dargan

by Phil Allcock

Trouble has darkened the skies of the Realm: the Golden Sceptre crafted by the hands of Elsinoth the Mighty has been stolen. Courageous twins, Kess and Linnil, team up with an assorted company of elves and crafters—and set out to find it.

Their journey takes them through rugged mountains, gentle valleys and wild woods to the grim stronghold of Dargan the Bitter. Will they win back the Sceptre? The answer depends on their courage, friendship and trust.

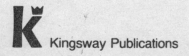

Kingsway Publications